Progressive
SAXOPHONE
METHOD
BOOK 1

by

Andrew Scott

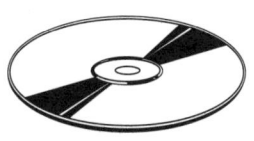

The exercises in this book have been recorded onto a CD

You can buy the CD direct from Koala Publications or from your local music store.

For further details on how to purchase this recording, or other books and CD's available in this series, contact:

KOALA PUBLICATIONS PTY LTD

37 Orsmond Street,
Hindmarsh,
South Australia 5007
AUSTRALIA

Ph: 61-8-8346 5366
Fax: 61-8-8340 9033

Email: info@koalapub.com.au

or visit our web page on:
www.koalapub.com.au

CD TRACK LISTING

1195

You Learn Faster When You Know How It Should Sound

All the exercises and songs in *Progressive Saxophone Method Book 1* have been recorded onto a stereo tape and C.D. which enables you to hear what you should be playing. This is a valuable method for learning quickly, and it also makes practicing more enjoyable, as you can play along with professional musicians from your very first lesson.

Each exercise has been recorded in stereo to enable you to listen to and play along with either

1. the saxophone by itself
    (balance control fully to the left), or

2. the saxophone with the backing instruments
    (balance control in the centre position), or

3. the backing instruments only
    (balance control fully to the right).

A drum is used to begin each exercise and to help you keep time.

There are two separate recordings – one for alto and baritone saxophones, and one for tenor and soprano saxophones. When you are ordering, be sure to let us know which recording you need.

Details on how to purchase the recordings are found on page 1 of this book.

Acknowledgements
Photographs by Phil Martin
Fingering diagrams by Garry Philip and James Stewart
Typesetting by Musictype Pty. Ltd.
Cover Instrument supplied by Silver Keys Music

I.S.B.N. 0 947183 04 3

ORDER CODES:

ALTO		TENOR	
Book	18304	Book	18304
CD Pack	CP-18304	CD Pack	CP-28304
CD Only	CD-18304	CD Only	CD-28304
Tape Only	T-18304	Tape Only	T-28304

Contents

Contents continued on next page

Contents (continued)

Introduction

Progressive Saxophone Method, consisting of two instruction books and a supplementary songbook, has been designed to introduce you to the basics of saxophone playing and reading music. To maximise your enjoyment and interest, the method incorporates an extensive repertoire of well-known songs. All the exercises and songs have been graded into an easy-to-follow, lesson-by-lesson format, which assumes no prior knowledge of music or the saxophone. Chord symbols for piano and guitar accompaniment are provided for each song and exercise.

Progressive Saxophone Method Book 1 incorporates very easy arrangements involving twelve natural notes, one sharp note, and one flat note. It introduces $\frac{4}{4}$ and $\frac{3}{4}$ time, whole, half, quarter and eighth notes and their equivalent rests, and describes in detail the correct procedure for breathing and blowing efficiently. You are taught how to read music, and introduced to such basic terms as bar lines, repeat signs and lead-in notes. The comprehensive glossary of musical terms will help you expand your knowledge of music, and the fingering index extends your range of notes to cover nearly three octaves.

Progressive Saxophone Method Book 2 contains more challenging arrangements of over forty songs, involving key signatures up to five sharps and two flats. The range of notes is extended up to D in the high register, and all the chromatic notes are introduced one by one. You are taught how to understand three new time signatures, ($\frac{2}{4}$, ¢ and $\frac{6}{8}$), how to recognise enharmonic notes and how to play syncopation in both straight and swing rhythms. You will also learn about sixteenth notes and become familiar with the rhythm created by the dotted eighth note-sixteenth note combination.

Progressive Saxophone Method Supplementary Songbook has been designed to be used in conjunction with the Method books. It contains more than 60 additional songs, which are cross referenced to the lessons in the Method Books.

Lesson One

How to Assemble the Saxophone

Step 1

Find all the parts that are shown below. The instrument shown here is an alto saxophone, but the procedure is similar for the other types of saxophone.

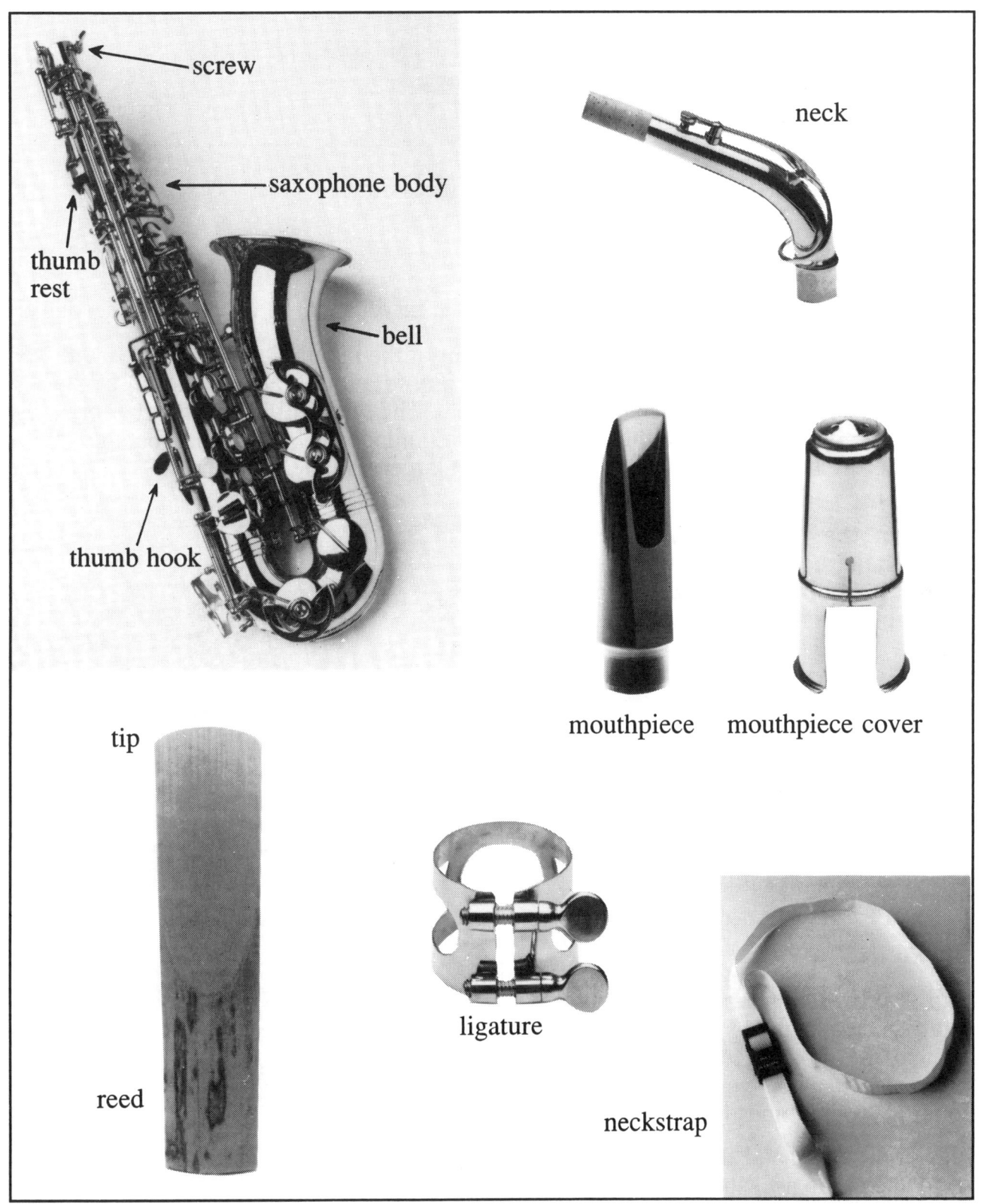

Step 2

Put the neckstrap around your neck.

Step 3

Attach the mouthpiece to the cork on the end of the neck. Use a twisting action. If it is tight, or makes a squeaking sound, you will need to apply some cork grease to the cork. (Cork grease is available from music stores).

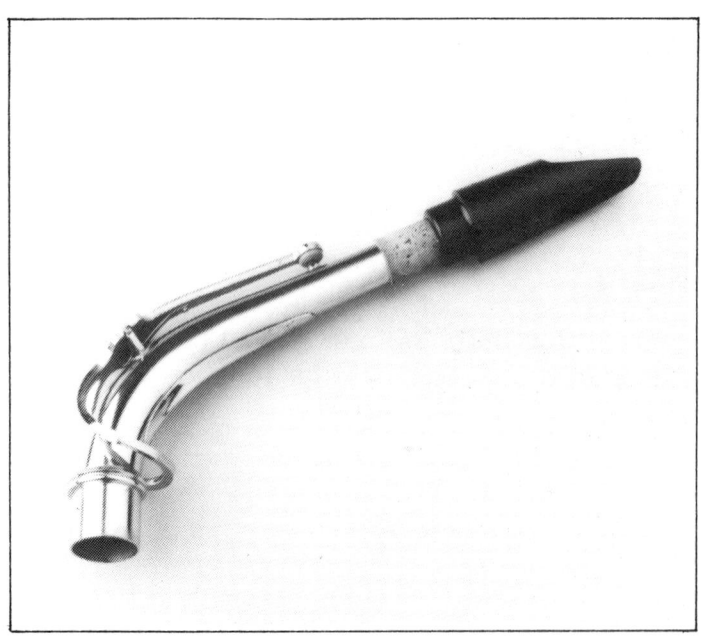

Push the mouthpiece on until it covers about three quarters of the cork.

Make sure that the flat part of the mouthpiece faces down.

Step 4

Moisten the reed by holding the thinner half of it in your mouth for about 15 seconds.

Place the flat part of the reed against the flat part of the mouthpiece and hold it with your thumb while you slide the ligature into place. Try to avoid touching the tip of the reed when you adjust it, otherwise you may damage it. The reed will have a number on it. The best reeds to start with are either a number 1 or a number $1\frac{1}{2}$. As the numbers get higher the reeds are harder to blow but they produce a larger volume of sound.

Position the reed so that there is just a hairline of black mouthpiece showing behind the reed. Tighten the ligature screws firmly.

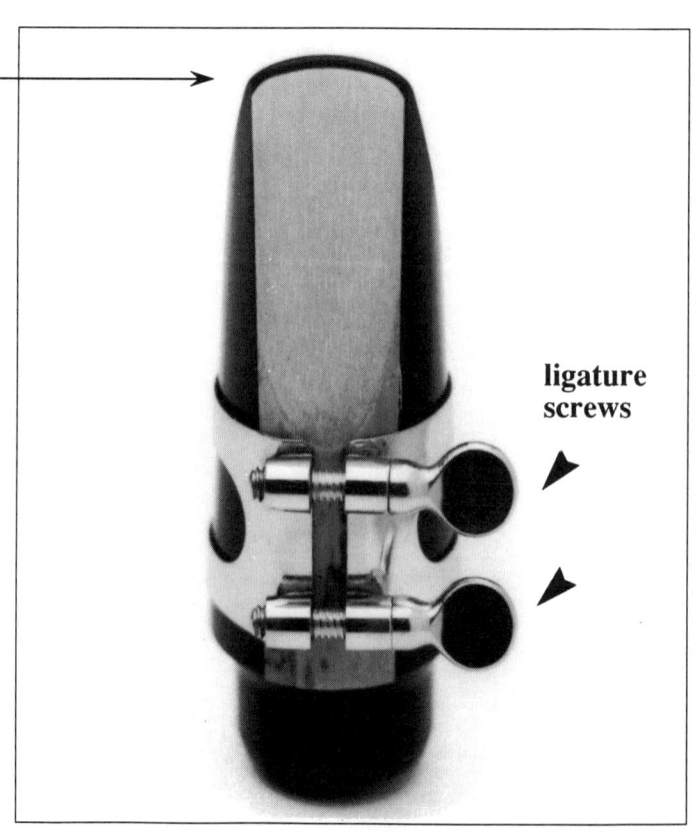

ligature screws

Step 5

Loosen the screw at the top of the saxophone body. Insert the neck into the body and line it up so that the neck points away from the bell. Tighten the screw. When you pick up the saxophone, lift it by the bell.

Step 6

Attach the saxophone to the neck strap and adjust the length of the strap so that the mouthpiece is level with your mouth when you are standing, looking straight ahead.

Use your right hand thumb to hold the saxophone away from your body, but don't lift with it. Let the neckstrap take all the weight.

How to Hold the Saxophone

Put your fingers on the G keys as shown in the diagram on page 8, with your left thumb on the thumb rest and your right thumb underneath the thumb hook.

Make sure your left hand is above the right.

How to Read the Fingering Diagram

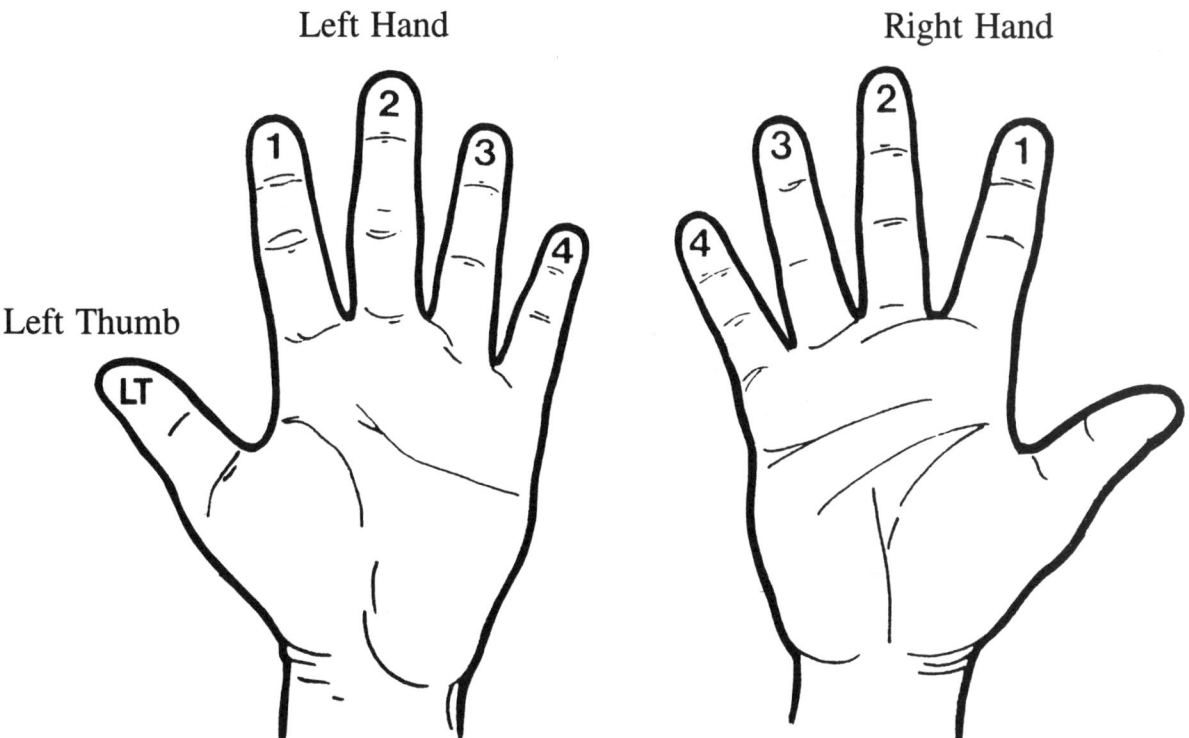

The numbers on the fingers correspond to the numbers and letters on the diagram on page 8.

Saxophone Fingering Diagram

The Note G

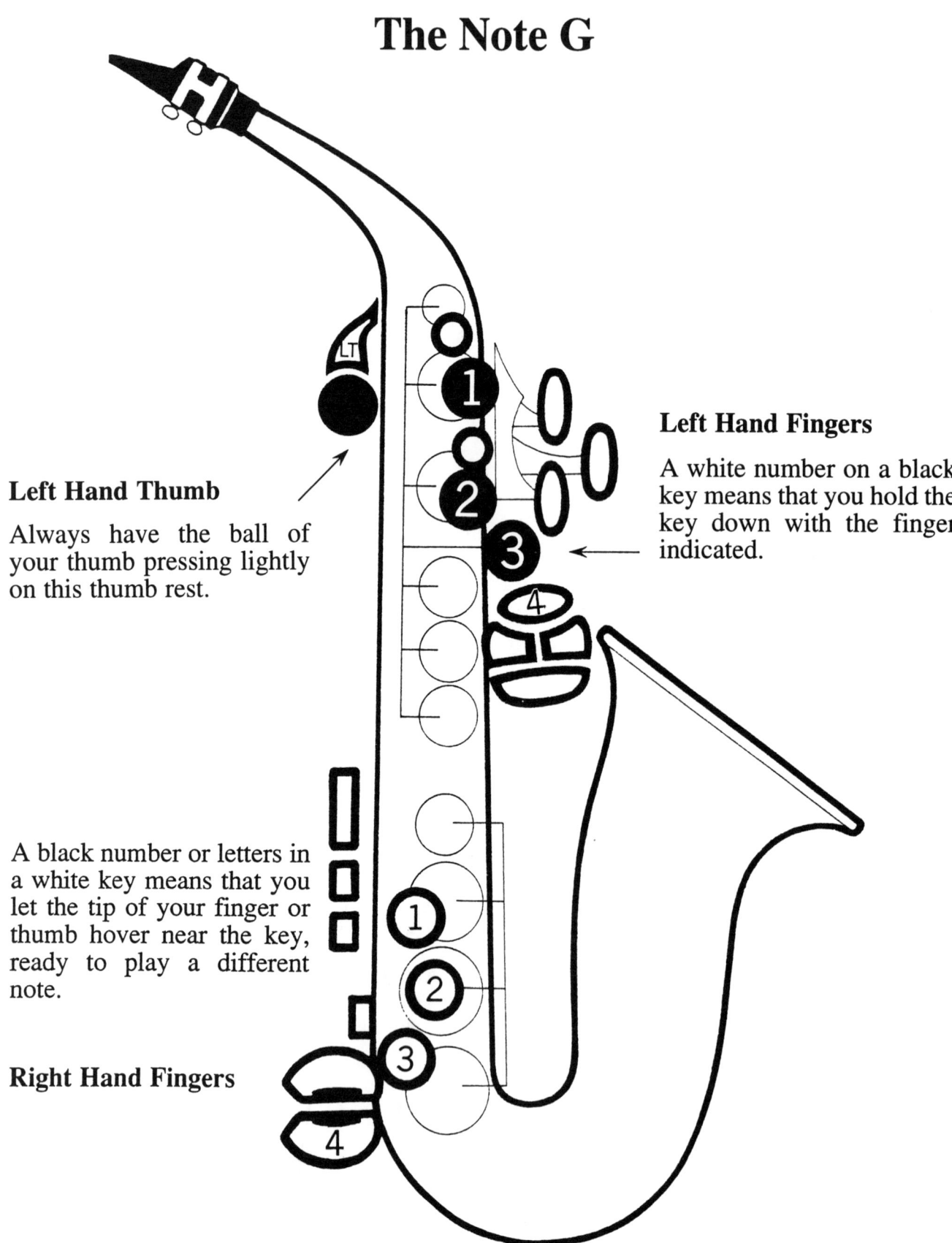

Left Hand Thumb

Always have the ball of your thumb pressing lightly on this thumb rest.

Left Hand Fingers

A white number on a black key means that you hold the key down with the finger indicated.

A black number or letters in a white key means that you let the tip of your finger or thumb hover near the key, ready to play a different note.

Right Hand Fingers

When your fingers are in the positions indicated here, you are fingering the note G.

How to Make a Sound

Put your fingers in position for the note G. Place your top teeth on the mouthpiece a little less than three eighths of an inch (one centimetre) from the end. Make an O shape with your mouth and cushion the reed gently with your lower lip, without turning your lower lip out or folding it in. Blow air through the saxophone until a note sounds. This is the note G.

Practice this several times until you can confidently play G.

Side view showing lower lip

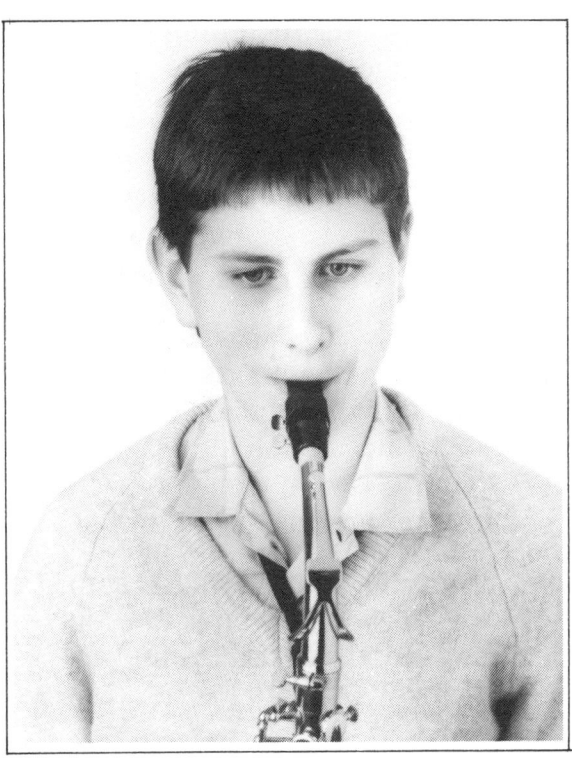
Front view

Tonguing

The notes will have a definite start and finish if you employ a technique known as **tonguing**. Without the saxophone, say the word "**doo**". Say it in a whisper. Notice that your tongue starts at the back of your top teeth, and you make the "**doo**" sound by quickly withdrawing it, a little like spitting.

Say "**doo**" again in a whisper, and this time follow through with your breath so that you create a continuous air stream. This is how you should start a note when you play the saxophone. Now with the saxophone in your mouth, let your tongue remain on the reed, closing off the gap in the mouthpiece, as you build up pressure in your mouth. Quickly release your tongue, and the note will start, definitely and crisply. To stop the note, simply put your tongue back on the reed. The note will stop immediately, and your tongue will be in position to start the next note.

Approach to Practice

It is better to practice in short blocks rather than for extensive periods without a break. The mind retains more information if it is allowed to rest between practice sessions. e.g., your learning will be more effective if you practice half an hour in the morning and half an hour in the afternoon than if you do one hour straight in the afternoon.

Lesson Two

How to Tune Your Saxophone to the Recording

1. Play your G note.

2. Start the recording and listen to the note that occurs at the beginning.

3. If the note on the recording sounds the same as your note, you are **in tune**. Proceed to the next page.

4. If the note on the recording sounds **higher (sharper)** than your note, your saxophone is **flat**. You will need to make it sharper by pushing the mouthpiece of your saxophone a little further onto the cork (about one eighth of an inch – three millimetres). Use a twisting action when you do this. Play your G again, then compare it with the recording. Keep doing this until your G sounds the same as the recording.

5. If the note on the recording sounds **lower (flatter)** than your note, your saxophone is **sharp**. You will need to make it flatter by pulling the mouthpiece of your saxophone a little further out along the cork (about one eighth of an inch – three millimetres). Play your G again, then compare it with the recording. Keep doing this until your G sounds the same as the recording.

6. As a final check, play your G at the same time as the note on the recording. If they are in tune, they will sound like one instrument. If not, there will be an unpleasant beating sound. Return to step 1.

Summary

To make the saxophone **SH**arper (**H**igher), make it **SH**orter.
To make the saxophone f**L**atter (**L**ower), make it **L**onger.

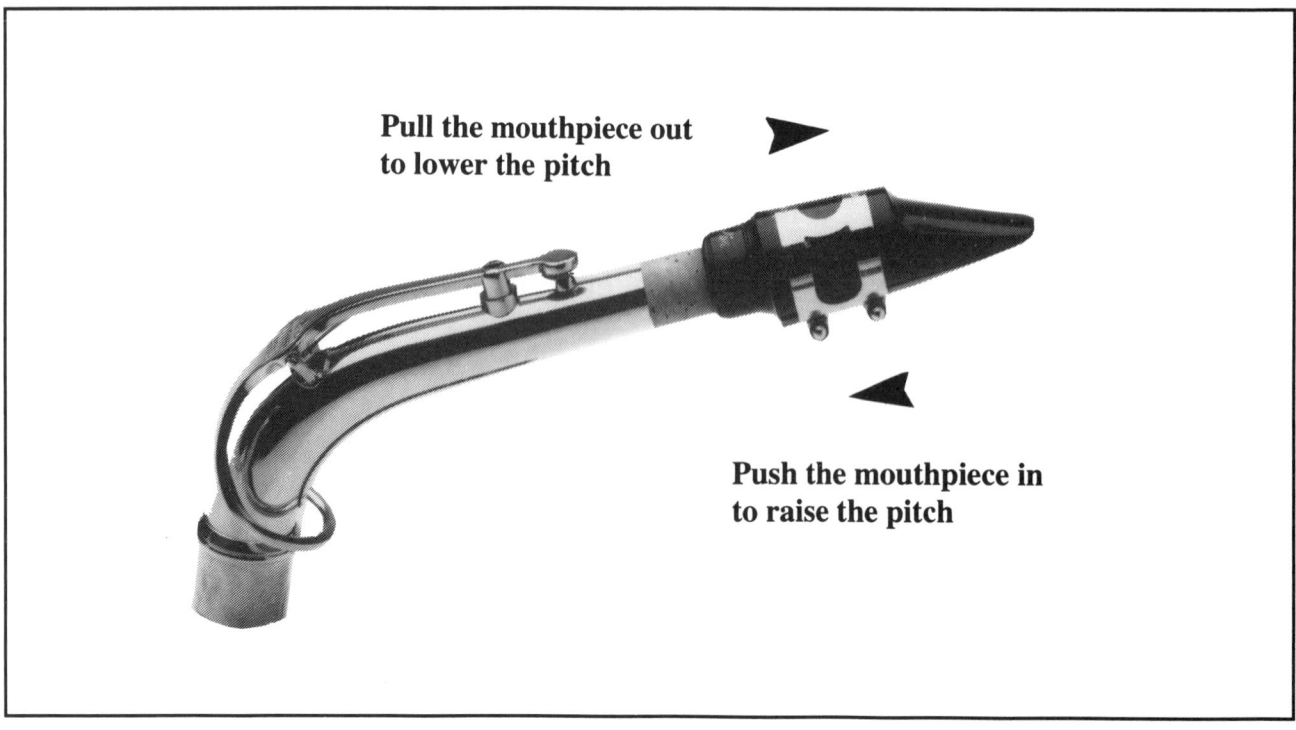

Pull the mouthpiece out to lower the pitch

Push the mouthpiece in to raise the pitch

How to Read Music

There are only seven letters used for notes in music. They are:

A B C D E F G

These notes are known as the **musical alphabet**.

The Staff

These five lines are called the **staff** or **stave**.

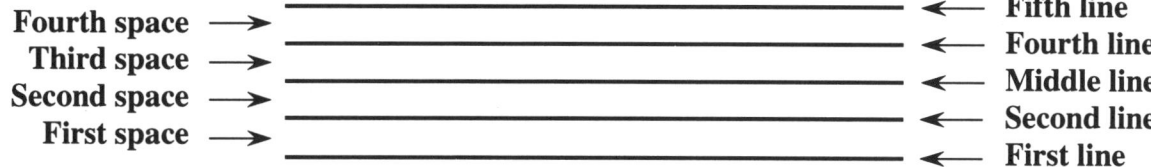

Fourth space →   ← Fifth line
Third space →   ← Fourth line
Second space →   ← Middle line
First space →   ← Second line
    ← First line

The Treble Clef

This symbol is called a **treble clef**. It dictates the position of notes on the staff.

There is a treble clef at the start of every line of saxophone music.

The Half Note

This is a music note called a **half note** (or **minim**). It has a value of **two** beats.

Count **1** 2

The Note G

Music notes are written in the spaces and on the lines of the staff. This note is a G note. It is written on the **second** line of the staff.

Bars

Music is divided into **bars** (or **measures**) by **bar lines**.

1 bar

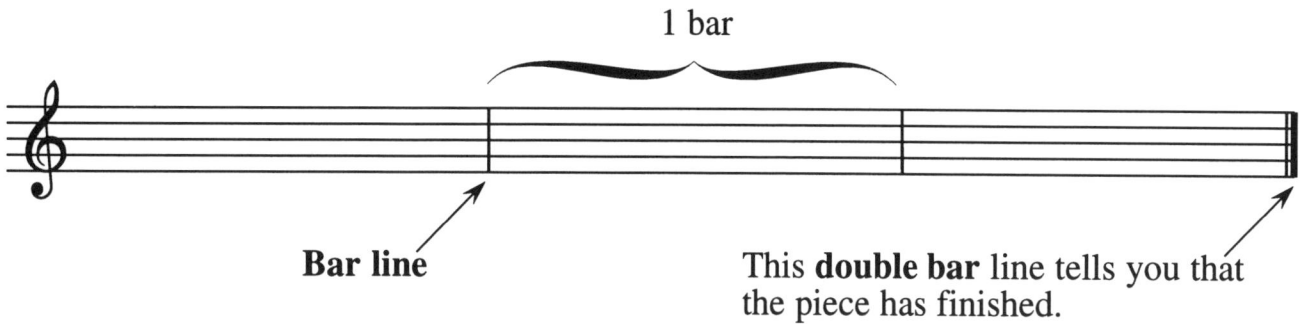

Bar line

This **double bar** line tells you that the piece has finished.

The Four Four Time Signature

These two numbers are called a **time signature**. They are placed after the treble clef.

The $\frac{4}{4}$ time signature tells you that there are **four** beats in each bar.

 **Exercise 1**

To play Exercise 1, count up to four before starting, to get the feel of the rhythm.

Think   – **one two** as you play the first G in each bar.
         – **three four** as you play the second G in each bar.

Tap your foot if it helps you count the beats.
Take a breath where you see this mark: ▼

On the recording there are **four** drumbeats to introduce exercises in $\frac{4}{4}$ time.

The letters above the staff are chord symbols, and are played by accompanying instruments, e.g. piano or guitar. The top chord is for instruments accompanying a **tenor** or **soprano** saxophone, the lower chord for instruments accompanying an **alto** or **baritone** saxophone.

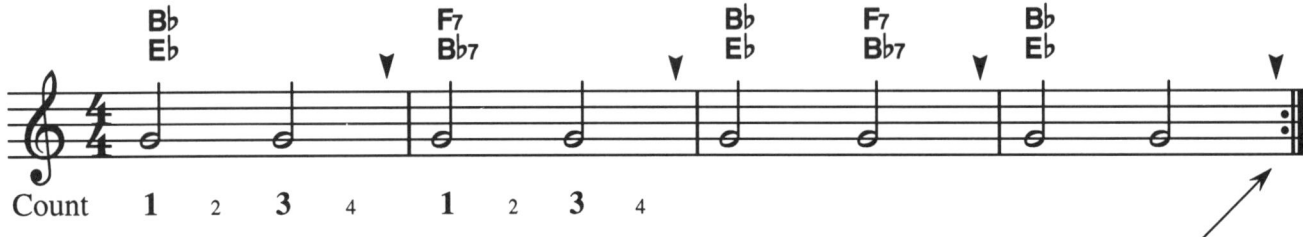

The big numbers **1** and **3** tell you to play the note. The small numbers 2 and 4 tell you to sustain it until the next note. Notice that there are four beats in each bar.

These two dots are called a **repeat sign**. This means that you play the exercise again from the start.

The Half Rest

This little black box is called a **half rest**, (or **minim rest**). It means **two** beats of silence. To play this rest, count for **two beats** without blowing.

 **Exercise 2**

Small counting numbers are used under rests.

Exercise 3

Count   1   2   3   4   1   2   3   4

The Quarter Note

This symbol is called a **quarter note** (or **crotchet**). It means play the note for **one** beat. Make sure you tongue each note.

Count **1**

Exercise 4

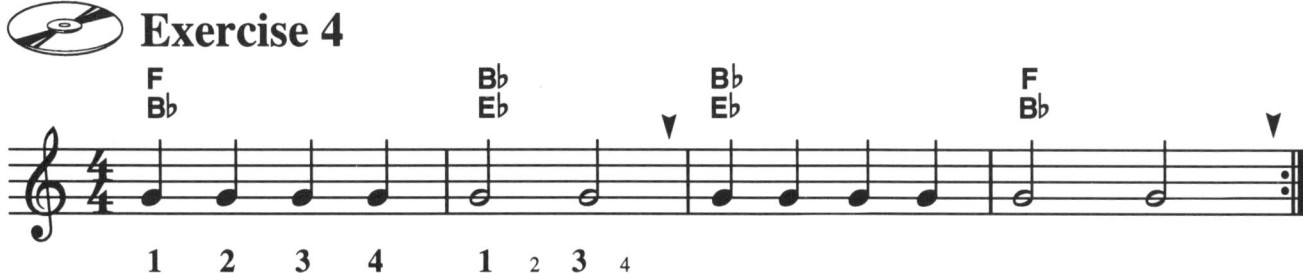

1   2   3   4   1   2   3   4

Tongue Tied

Quarter notes and half notes can be combined in one bar so that each bar has a total of **four** beats.

Only one bar line means continue to the next line of music.

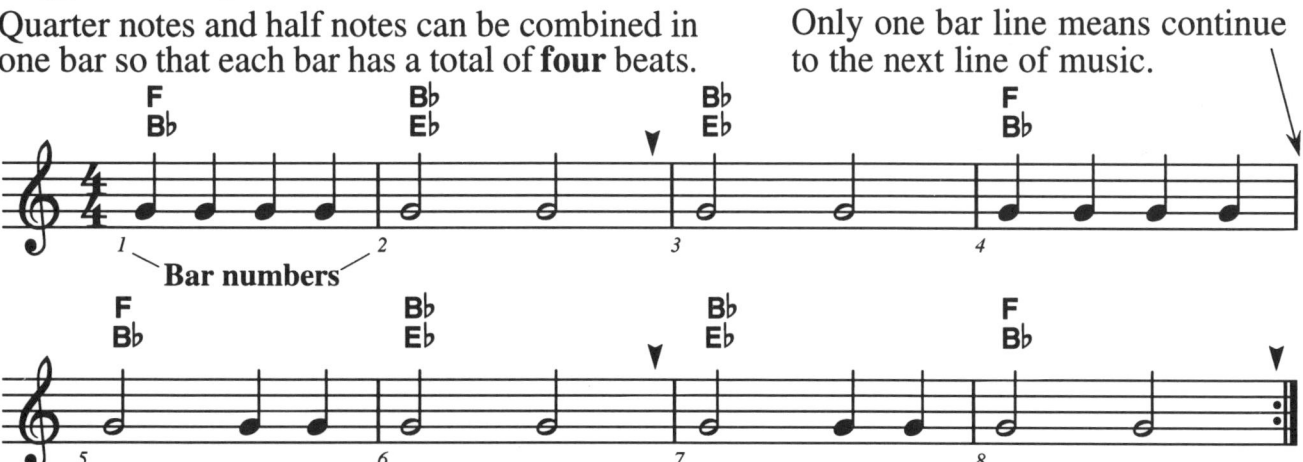

Bar numbers

The Quarter Rest

This symbol is a **quarter rest** (or **crotchet rest**). It means one beat of silence. To play this rest, count for one beat without blowing.

Count 1

Exercise 5

Count   1   2   3   4   1   2   3   4   1   2   3   4   1   2   3   4

14

 **Rest Easy**

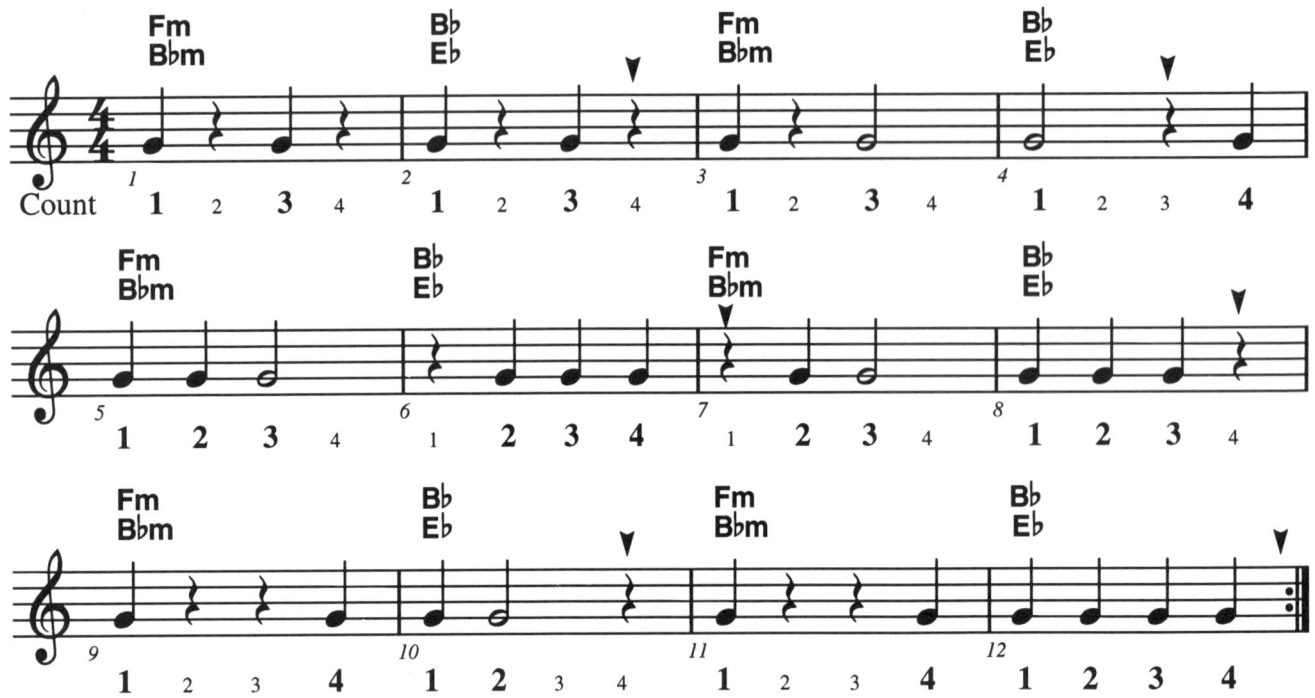

How to Clean the Saxophone

1. Tie one end of a piece of string around the corner of a soft rag. Tie the other end to a non-scratching weight.

2. Dismantle the saxophone and drop the weight into the bell.

3. Tip the saxophone upside down so that the weight falls out the neck. Pull the rag through the instrument a few times, thus cleaning and drying it.

4. Do the same with the neck.

5. Wash the mouthpiece in warm water and dry it.

6. Don't mind about scratch marks on top of the mouthpiece (unless you're playing a rented saxophone). They will develop into a comfortable groove for your teeth to rest in.

Lesson Three

The Note A

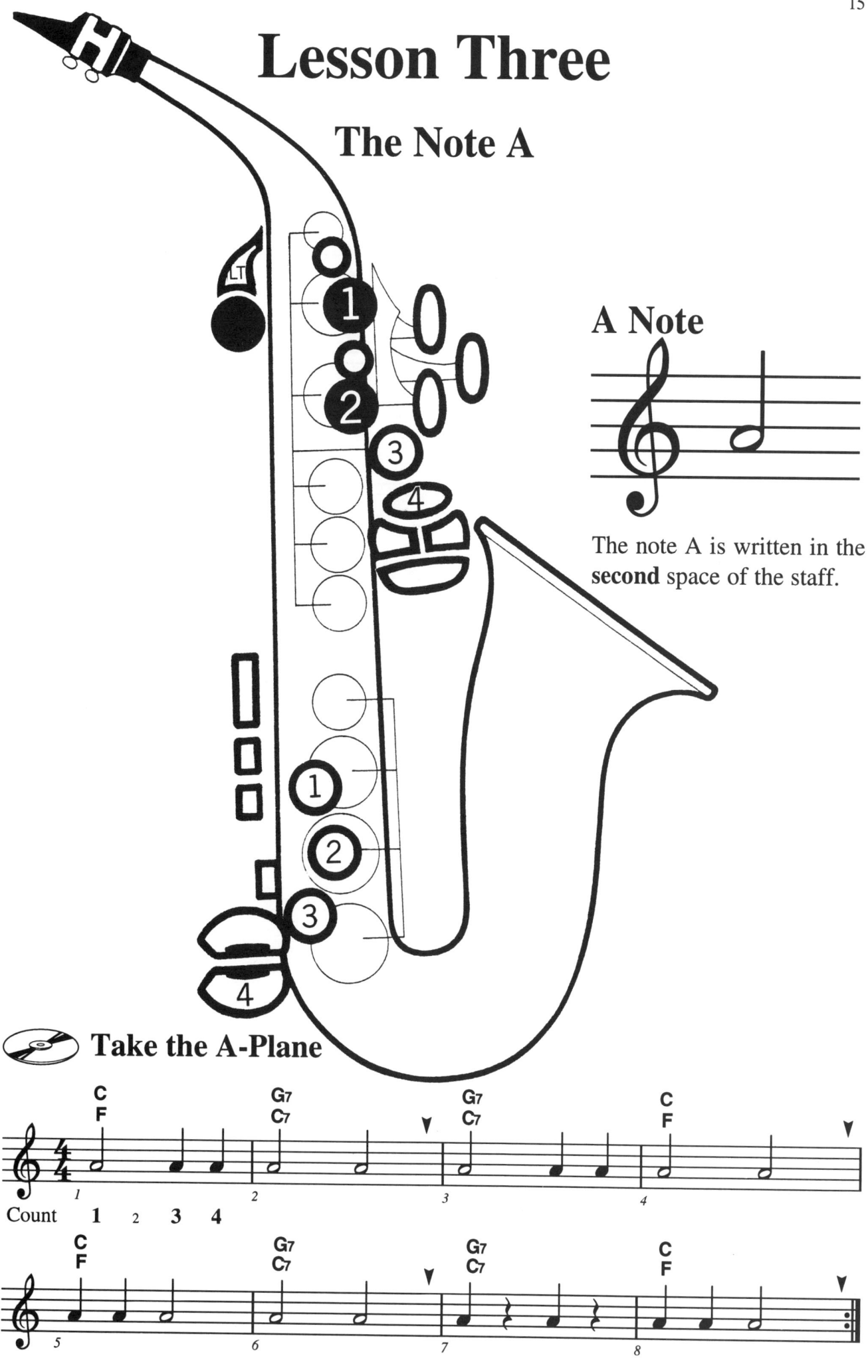

A Note

The note A is written in the **second** space of the staff.

Take the A-Plane

 Two Note Samba

In this song you use the two notes you have learnt so far. The first and second fingers of your left hand stay on the keys for both notes. Lift your third finger off to change from G to A.

Two Blue

This song is a **duet** - a piece for two instruments. The student plays the top line and the teacher plays the bottom line. Practice playing your part along with the teacher's part on the recording.

The Note B

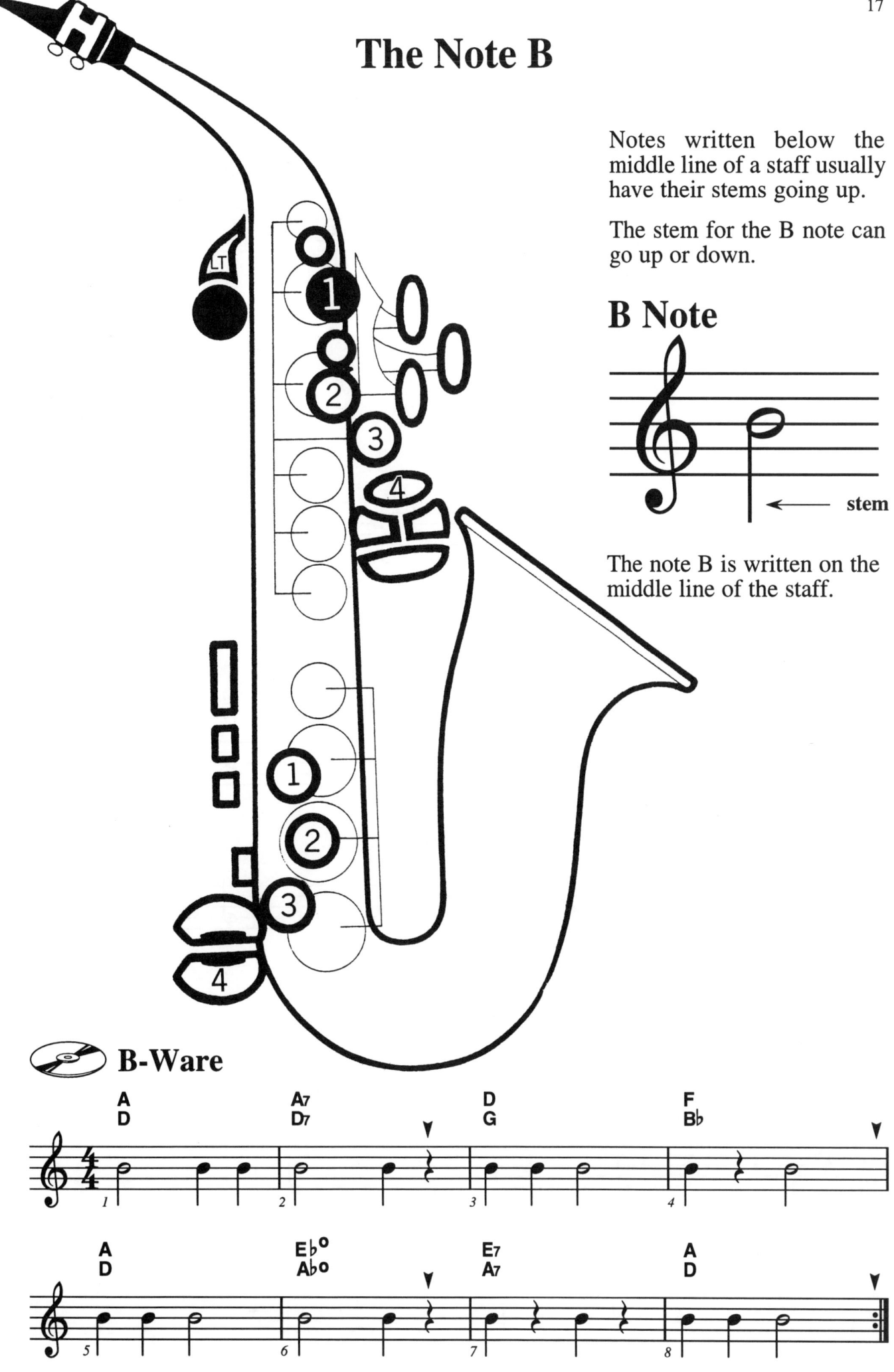

Notes written below the middle line of a staff usually have their stems going up.

The stem for the B note can go up or down.

B Note

The note B is written on the middle line of the staff.

B-Ware

18

 ## Exercise 6

If you have trouble distinguishing the notes from each other, write their names below the staff, as in Exercise 6.

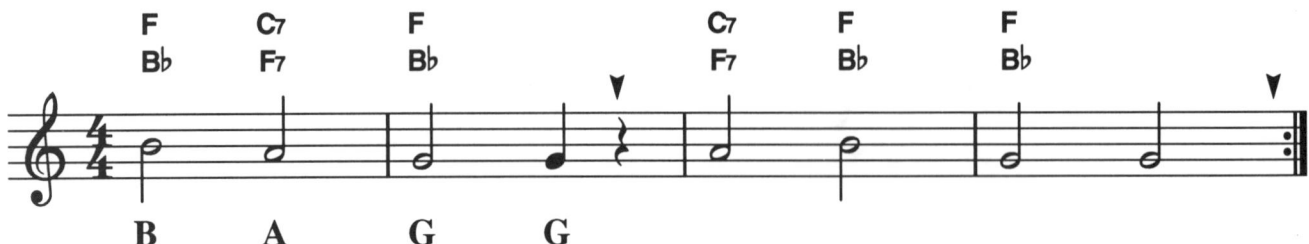

 ## Exercise 7

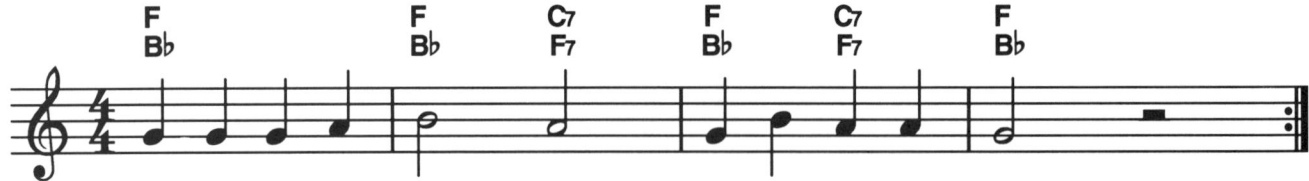

 ## Mixed Bag

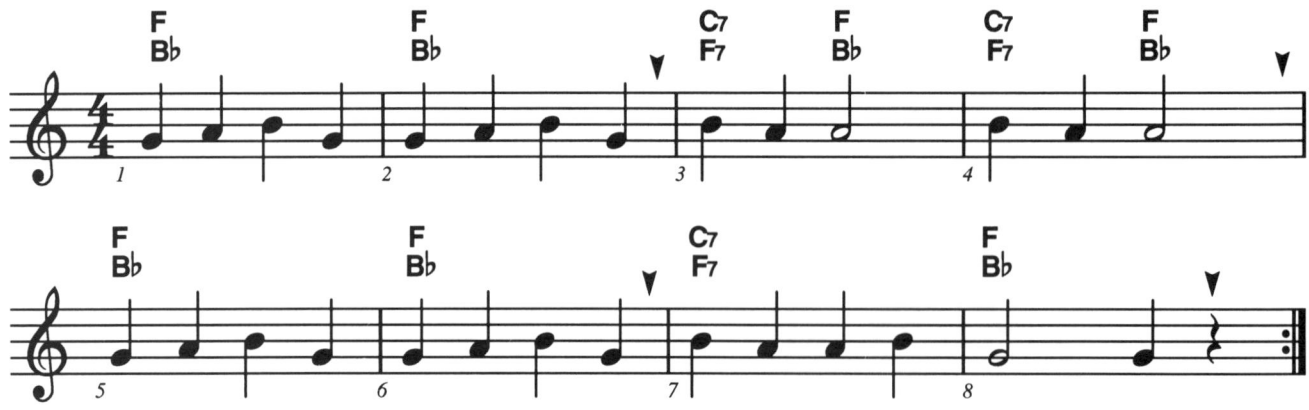

Rock Solid

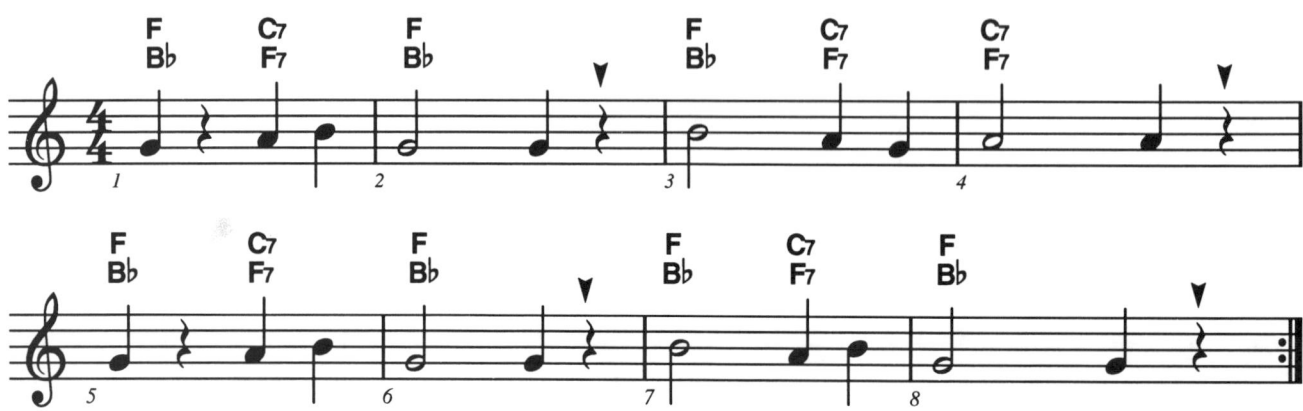

Lesson Four

The Note C

Notes written above the middle line of a staff usually have their stems going down.

C Note

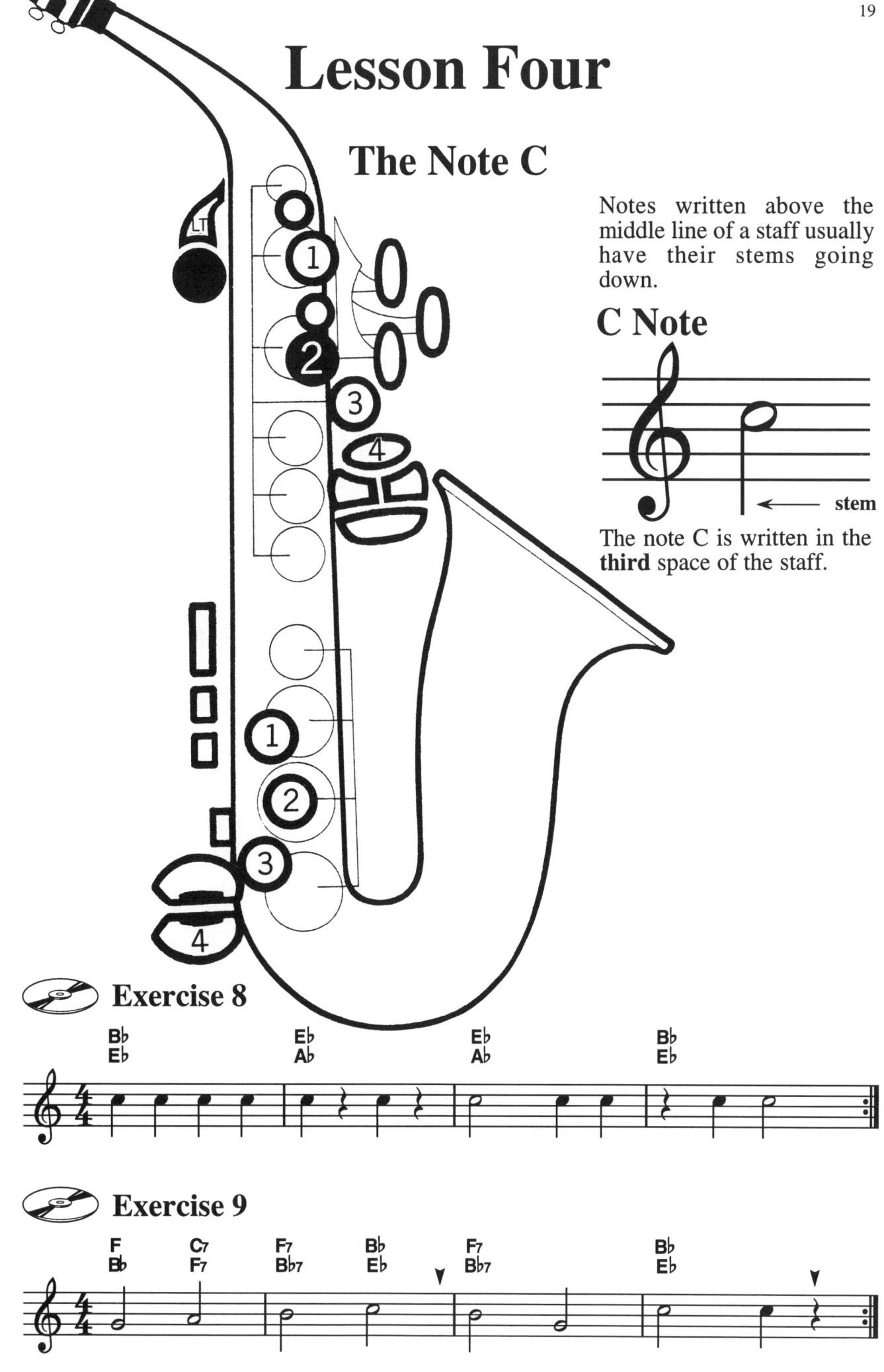

← **stem**

The note C is written in the **third** space of the staff.

Exercise 8

| B♭ | E♭ | E♭ | B♭ |
| E♭ | A♭ | A♭ | E♭ |

Exercise 9

| F | C7 | F7 | B♭ | F7 | B♭ |
| B♭ | F7 | B♭7 | E♭ | B♭7 | E♭ |

Easy to C

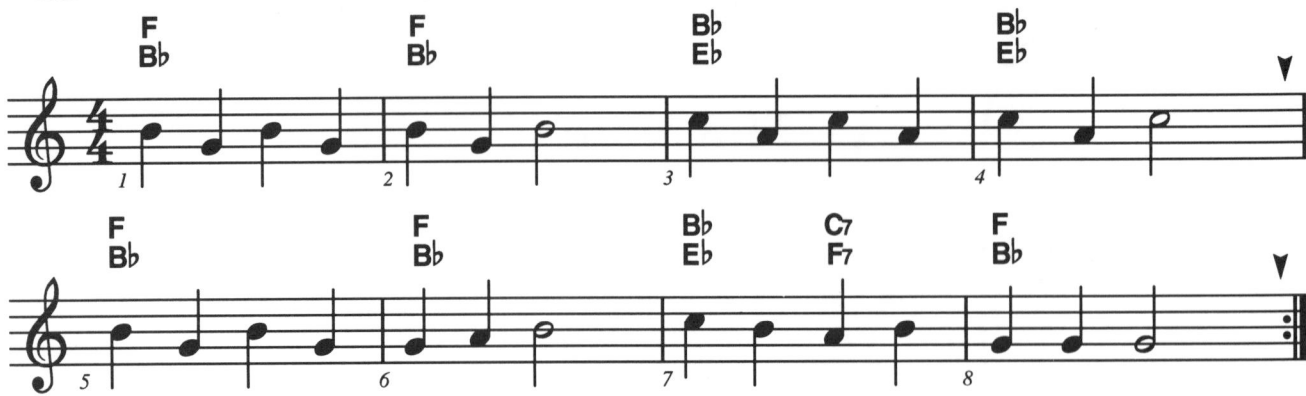

The Dotted Half Note

A **dot** written after a note lengthens its value by a half. A dot placed after a half note means that you hold the note for **three** beats.

1 beat quarter note	**2 beats** half note	**3 beats** dotted half note

Crystal Rock

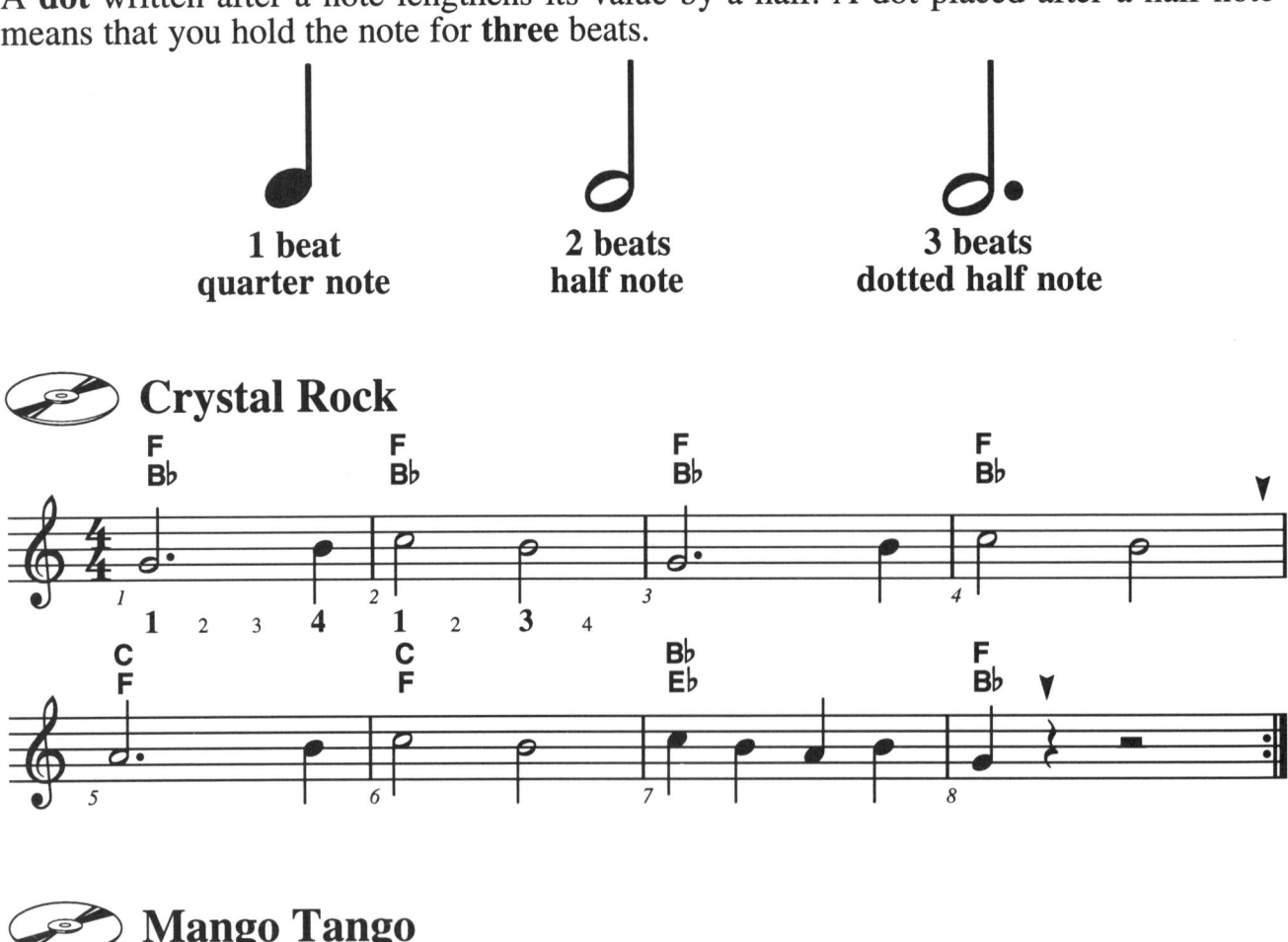

Mango Tango

The Three Four Time Signature

The $\frac{3}{4}$ after the treble clef means that there are only **three** beats in each bar. This gives the rhythm a completely different feel to $\frac{4}{4}$ time.

$\frac{3}{4}$ is also known as **waltz** time.

 Three's a Crowd

On the recording there are **three** drumbeats to introduce songs in $\frac{3}{4}$ time.

 Barcarolle

Jacques Offenbach

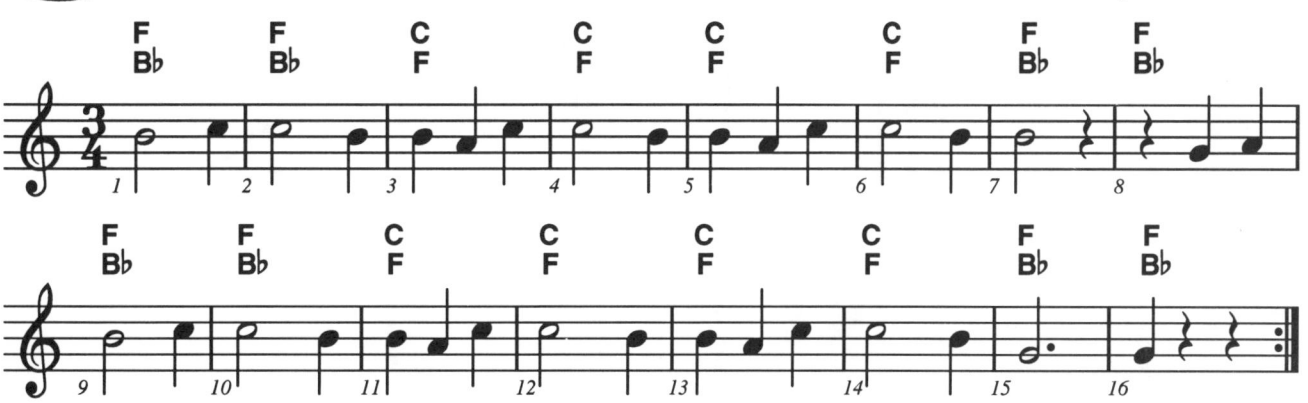

Opera House Waltz

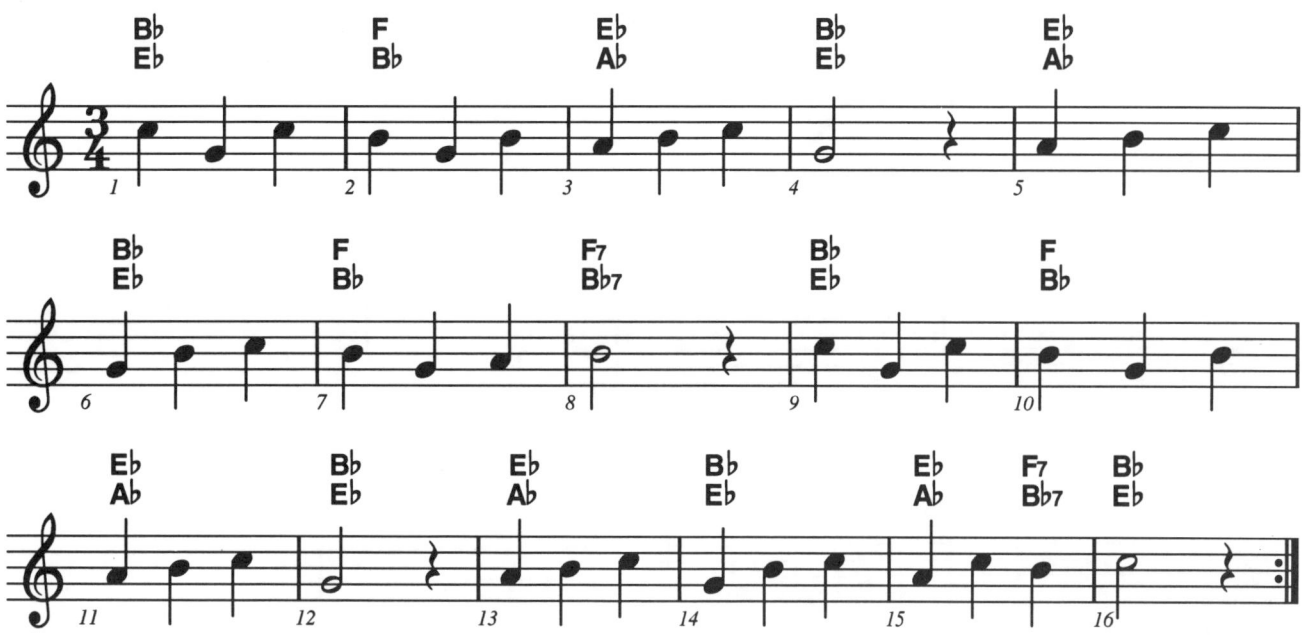

Lesson Five

The Note F

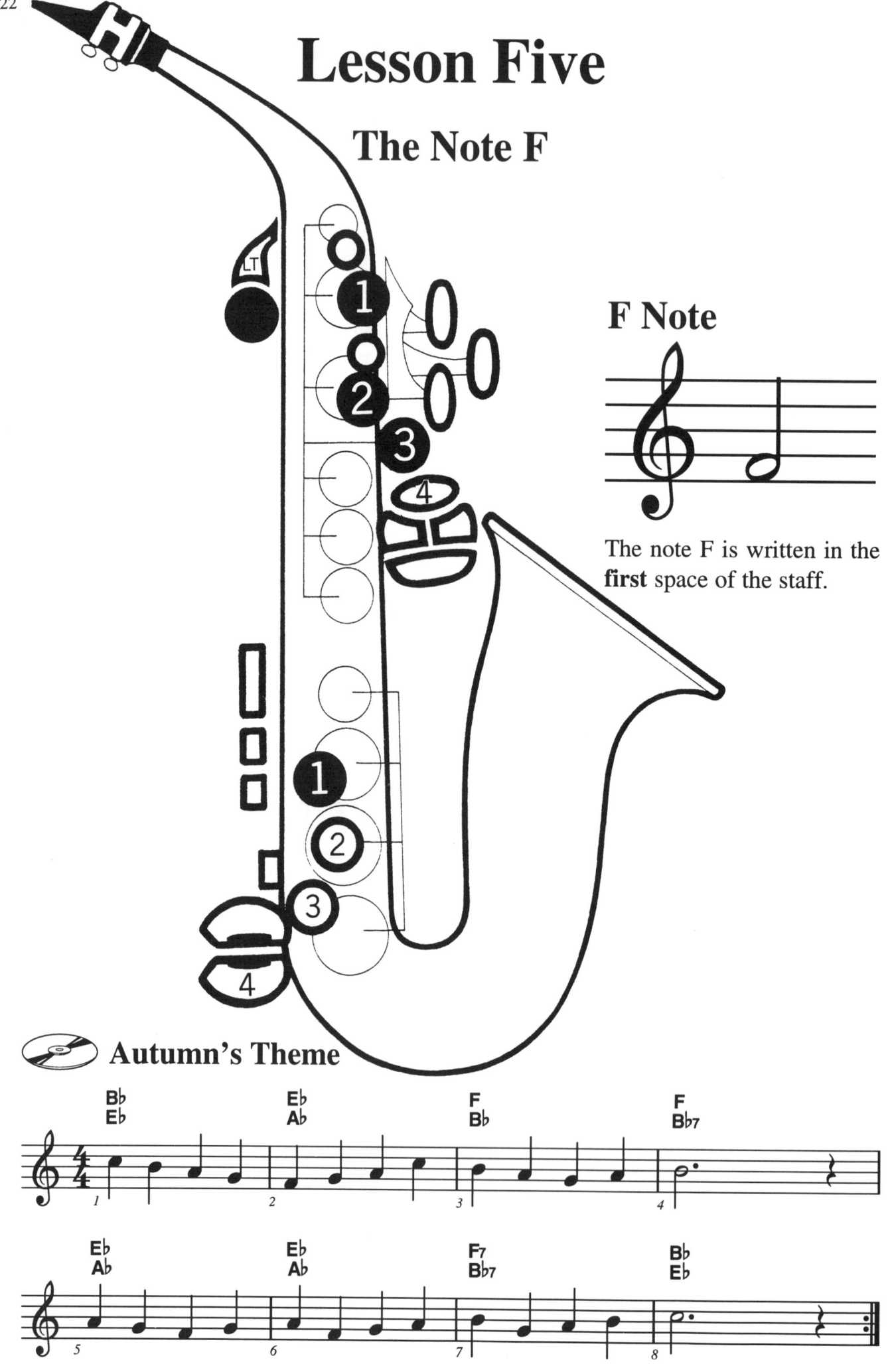

F Note

The note F is written in the **first** space of the staff.

Autumn's Theme

The Slur

 Exercise 10

The **slur** is a curved line drawn above (or below) two or more different notes. It tells you to play the notes smoothly. Playing smoothly is called **legato**. To play the notes smoothly, only tongue the first note of the group and keep blowing while you change your fingers.

Tongue only the **first** note.

To Slur with Love

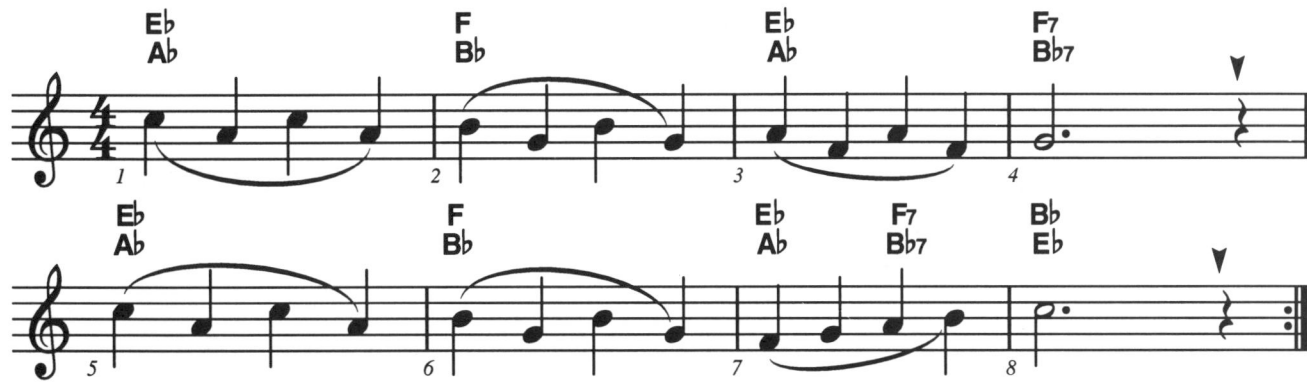

Orange Blossom

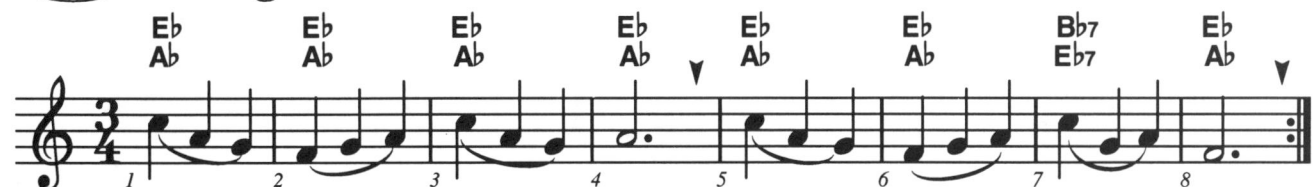

Staccato

 Exercise 11

A dot placed above or below a note tells you to play the note **staccato**. Staccato means to play a note short and separate from other notes. To play a note short, make a "d" action with your tongue, instead of the longer "doo" action.

Staccato is the opposite of legato.

CC Senor

This song combines staccato and legato.

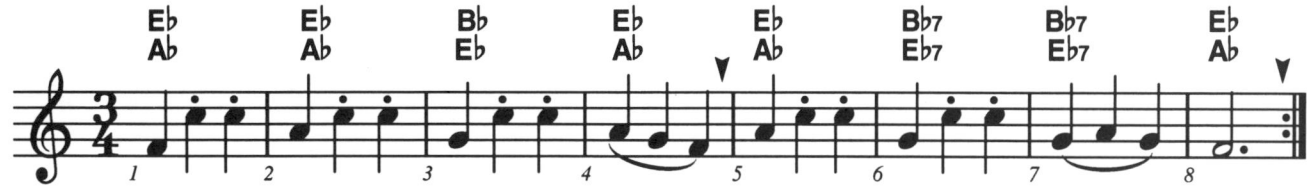

Lesson Six

The Note B Flat (B♭)

Flat Signs

♭ This is a **flat** sign.

A flat sign lowers the pitch of the note to which it applies by an **interval** (see glossary) known as one **semitone** or one **half step**. Thus the note B♭ is one semitone **lower** than B. Since the difference in pitch between the notes A and B is one whole tone (two semitones or one **whole step**), B♭ is also one semitone **higher** than A.

B♭ (B Flat) Note

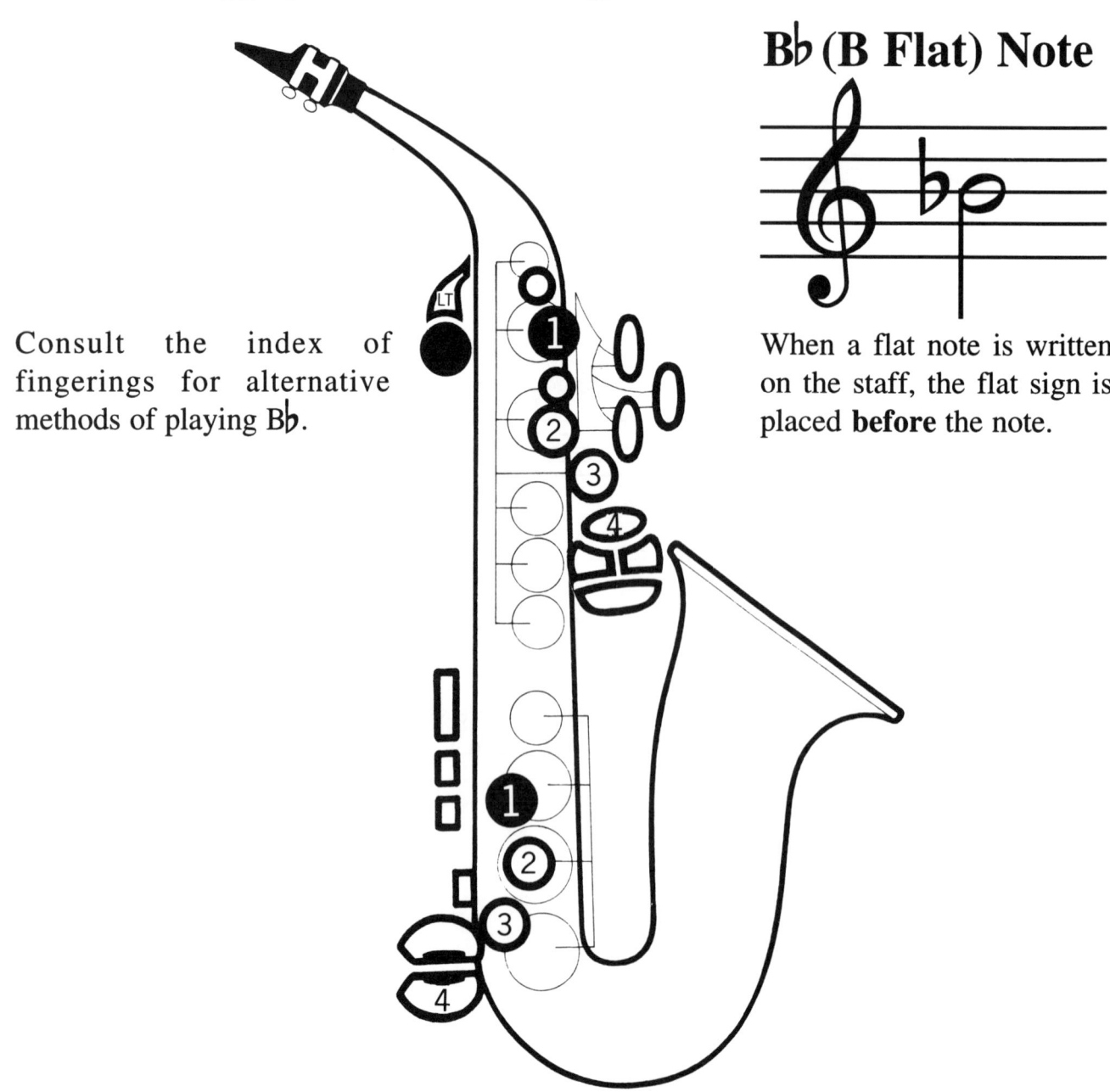

Consult the index of fingerings for alternative methods of playing B♭.

When a flat note is written on the staff, the flat sign is placed **before** the note.

Exercise 12

Instead of writing a flat sign before every B♭ note, it is easier to write just one flat sign after the treble clef. This means that all B notes on the staff are played as B♭, even though there is no flat sign placed before the note.

Ode to Joy

Ludwig van Beethoven

The Common Time Signature

C This symbol is called **common time**. It means exactly the same as $\frac{4}{4}$ time.

Mambo Jumbo

Aura Lee

Traditional

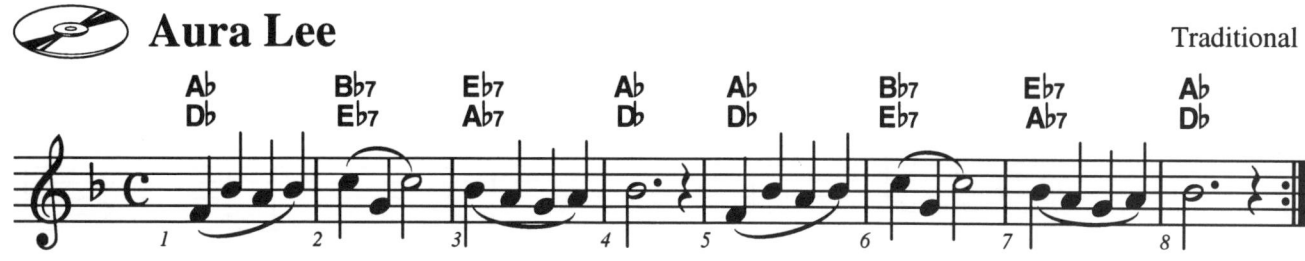

German Drinking Song

Traditional German

The Tie

Exercise 13

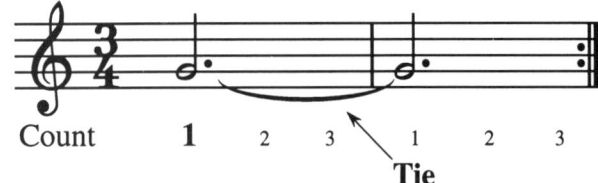

A **tie** is a curved line that connects two notes with the same position on the staff. The tie tells you to tongue the first note only, and to hold it for the length of both notes.

Beautiful Brown Eyes

Traditional

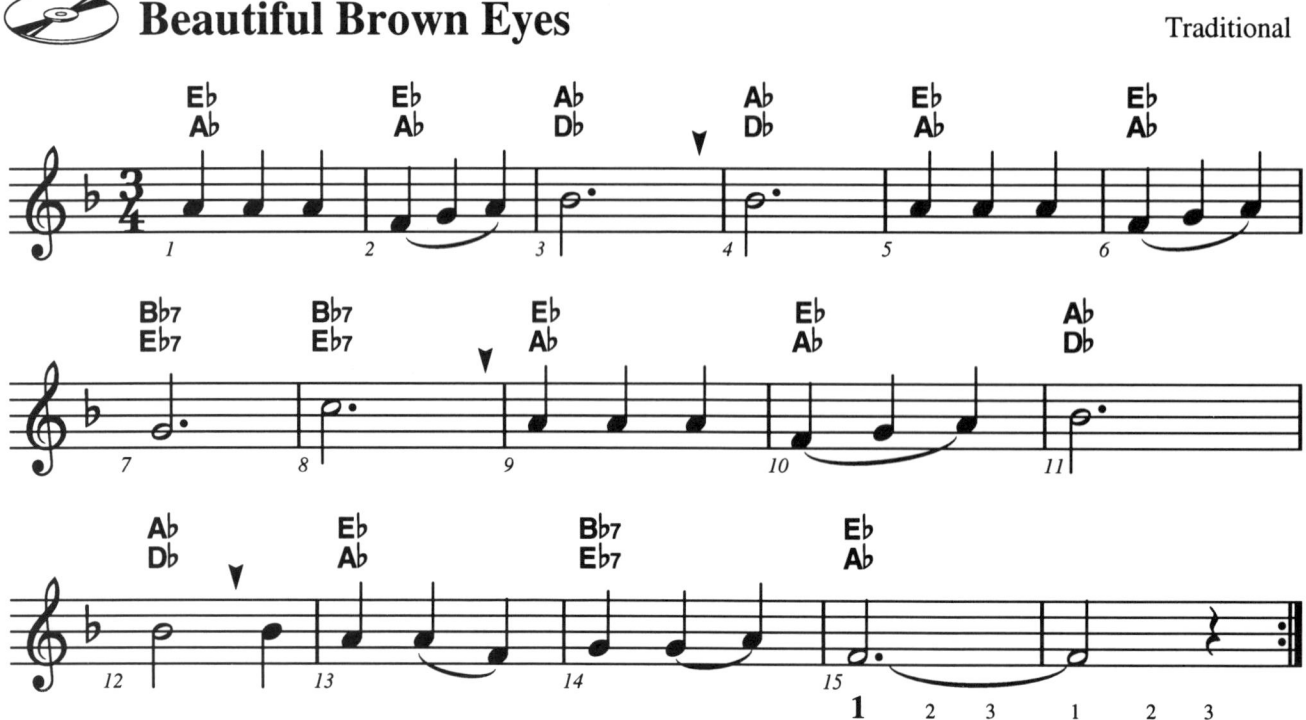

Roses from the South

Johann Strauss

The Whole Note

This is a **whole note** (or **semibreve**).
It lasts for **four** beats.
There is one whole note in one bar of $\frac{4}{4}$ time.

Good Evening Friends

Count   1   **2**   **3**   **4**   **1**   2   3   4

Lesson Seven

The Lead-in (or Pick-up)

Sometimes a song does not begin on the first beat of a bar. Any notes which come before the first full bar are called **lead-in notes** (or **pick-up notes**). When lead-in notes are used the last bar is also incomplete. The notes in the lead-in and the notes in the last bar add up to one full bar.

The Banks of the Ohio

Traditional

On the recording there are **five** drumbeats to introduce this song.

The Mexican Hat Dance

Traditional Mexican

On the recording there are **five** drumbeats to introduce this song.

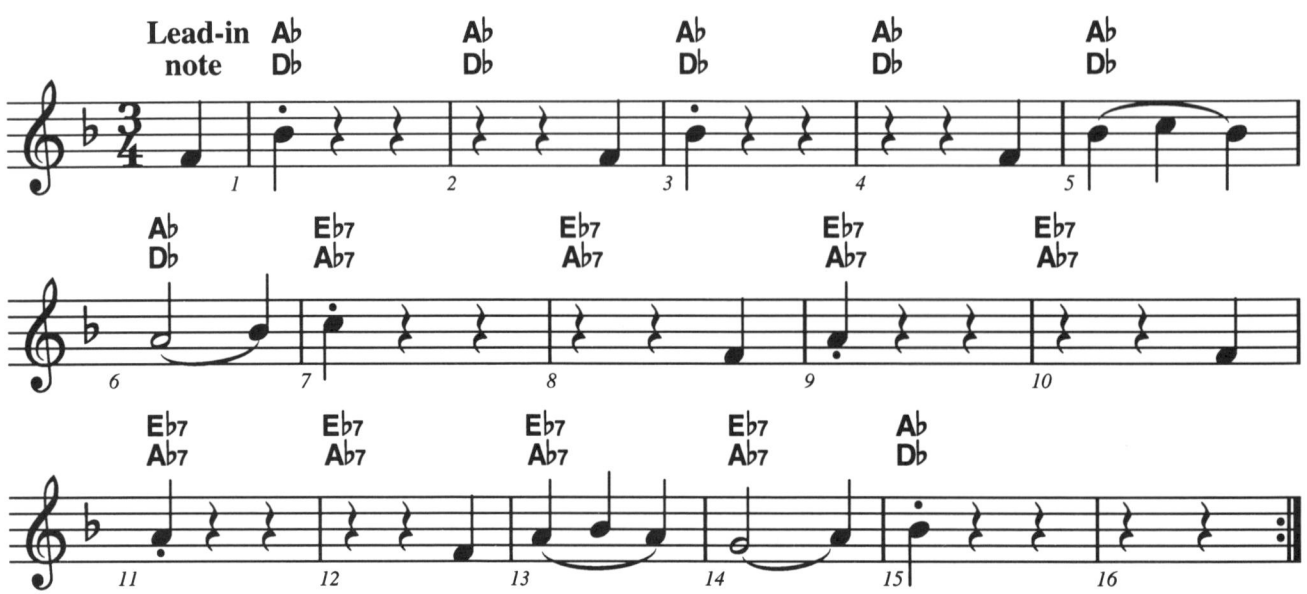

When the Saints Go Marchin' In

Traditional

On the recording there are **five** drumbeats to introduce this song.

Lesson Eight

The Power Blowing Technique

It is best if you have a teacher to help you understand this section.

Step 1

Lie on your back on the floor, legs straight out. Place the palm of one hand over your navel. Make as if you are blowing your nose. Feel your muscles tighten underneath your hand as you do this. Continue blowing until the muscles are quite tight. Hold them tight for a few seconds. By this time you really need a breath. Let go those muscles you were blowing out with. Notice that your hand moves up and you get bigger round the waist as your new breath fills your lungs. Just relax your abdominal muscles and you will breathe in automatically.

Step 2

Repeat **Step 1**. Observe that blowing out equals effort, and breathing in equals relaxation. Now blow out through your mouth, very gently and slowly. Shape your lips as if you are playing the saxophone. Breathe in and out, over and over, until you think you understand.

Step 3

Stand up and go through the cycle again. Don't try to suck air in. Think of an inflatable life-raft - you pull out the plug and Floop!, it fills up by itself.

Step 4

Play the exercises on the saxophone. Take breaths at the places marked, even if you don't need to.

Remember: Breathe in   -   Relax
Blow out   -   Tighten

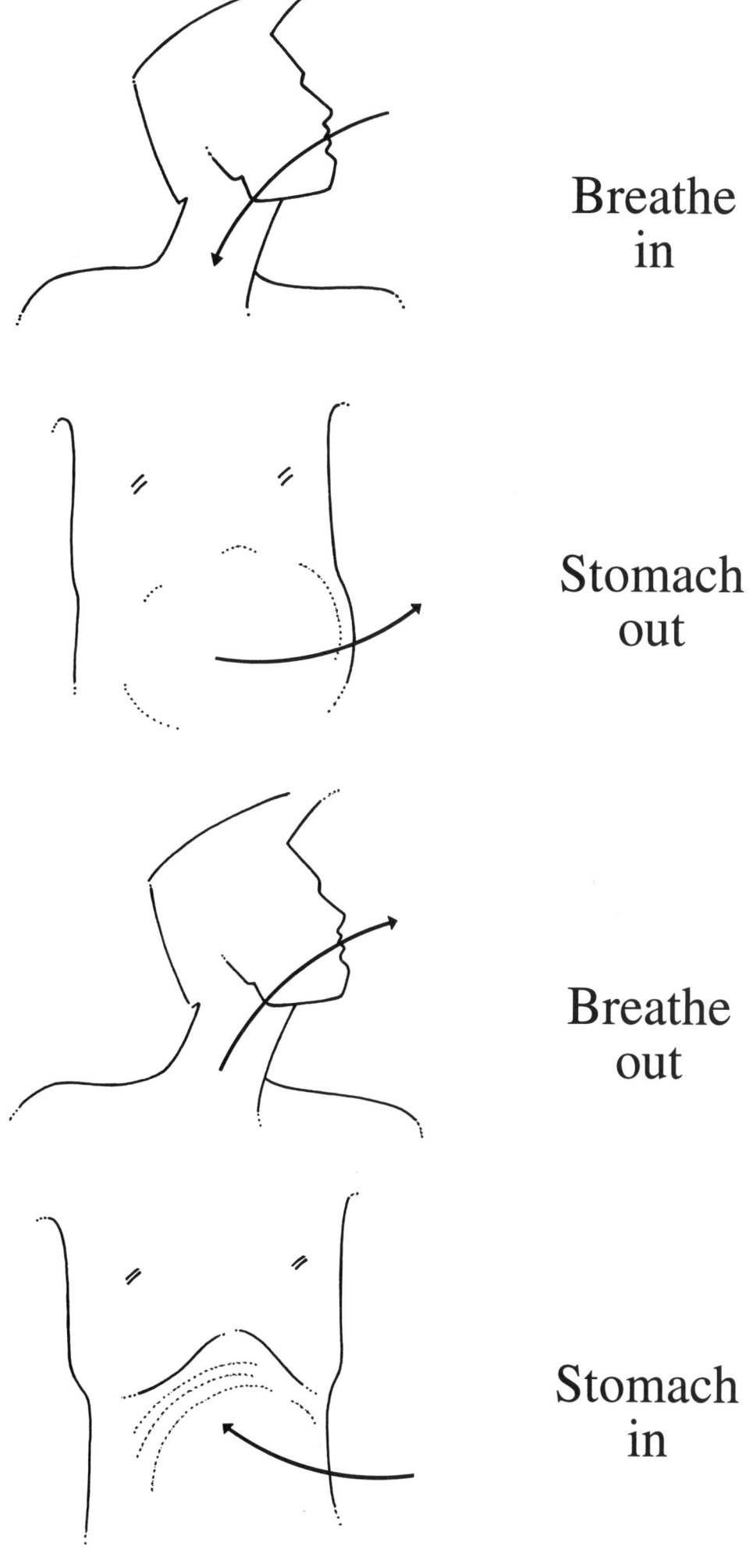

Breathe
in

Stomach
out

Breathe
out

Stomach
in

Exercise 17

Exercise 18

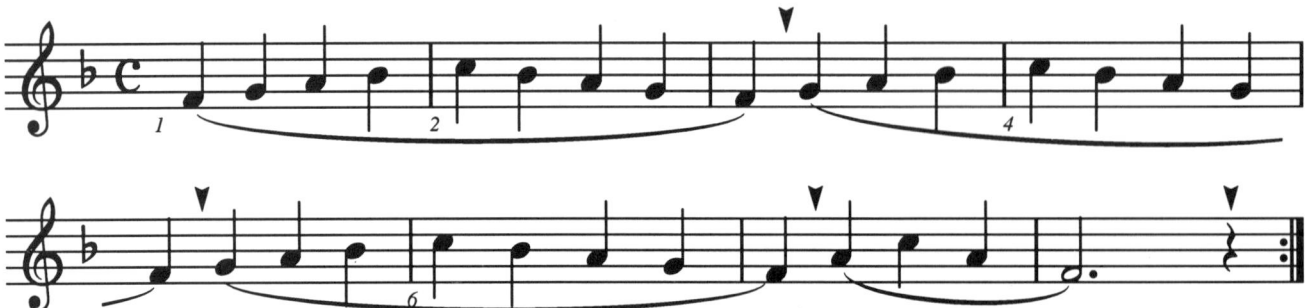

Exercise 19

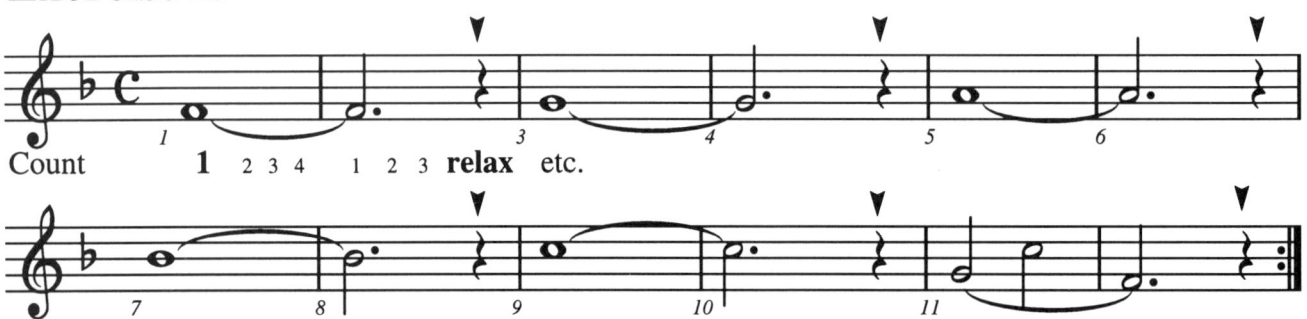

Count   **1**   2 3 4   1   2 3 **relax**   etc.

Helpful Hints

1. The more you can relax, the deeper your in-breath will be.
2. When you blow out, think of a tube of toothpaste. If you squeeze it from the bottom, you use all the tooth-paste. But, if you squeeze from the top, some remains in the bottom. So it is with your lungs. Gently squeeze from your abdominal area and all the air will be used and you'll have more control.
3. This is yoga breathing.
4. When you use this method, you fill up your lungs from the very bottom. The breaths will be deeper and quicker than before.
5. The process may seem contrary to everything you have learnt in life about breathing. If it is, good. You will be more healthy as a result of learning this. When you have mastered it, you will see how natural it is. You will find yourself breathing this way 24 hours a day.
6. You may not see much movement of your belly at first when you breathe in. When you can relax those muscles more fully, there will be more motion visible.
7. Practice the technique at other times, walking, waiting for the bus, driving. No-one will be able to tell.

               Remember this above all else:
               Breathe in   =   **Relax**
               Blow out   =   **Gentle effort**

When you are doing it right, it gets easier and easier.

Lesson Nine

The Note E

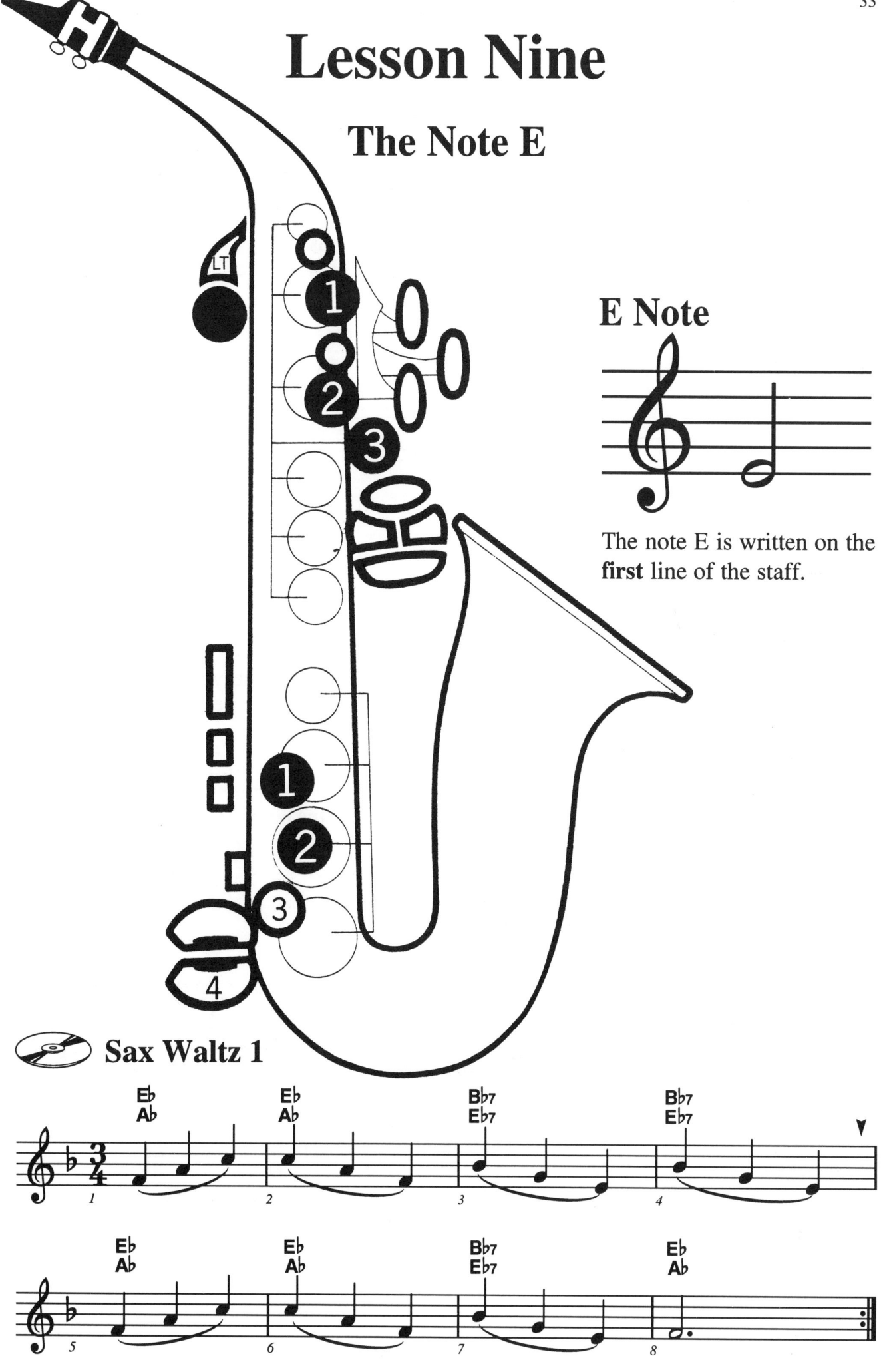

E Note

The note E is written on the **first** line of the staff.

Sax Waltz 1

Mary Ann

Traditional

First and Second Endings

The next song contains **first and second endings**. The first time you play through the song, play the first ending then go back to the beginning. The second time you play through the song, play the second ending instead of the first.

In Sax Waltz 2 play through to the end of the first ending (bar 8), then repeat the song from the beginning as indicated by the repeat dots. When you play through the song the second time, do not play bars 7 and 8 again (the first ending), but play bars 9 and 10 (the second ending).

Sax Waltz 2

Lesson Ten

Tail

The Eighth Note

This is an **eighth** note (or **quaver**). There are eight eighth notes in one bar of $\frac{4}{4}$ time. When eighth notes are joined together, the tails are replaced by one **beam**.

← Beam

Two eighth notes joined together.

Four eighth notes joined together.

How to Count Eighth Notes

 **Exercise 20**

$B\flat$
$E\flat$ } throughout

Count 1 + 2 + 3 + 4 +   1   2 + 3   4 +   1 + 2 + 3 + 4 +   1   2 + 3   4
Think   one and two and three and four and etc.

 **Shave and a Haircut**   Traditional

Count 1   2 + 3   4   1   2   3

 **Rock Riff 1**

 **Mick's Mexican Mix**   Traditional

On the recording there are **five** drumbeats to introduce this song.

The Note D

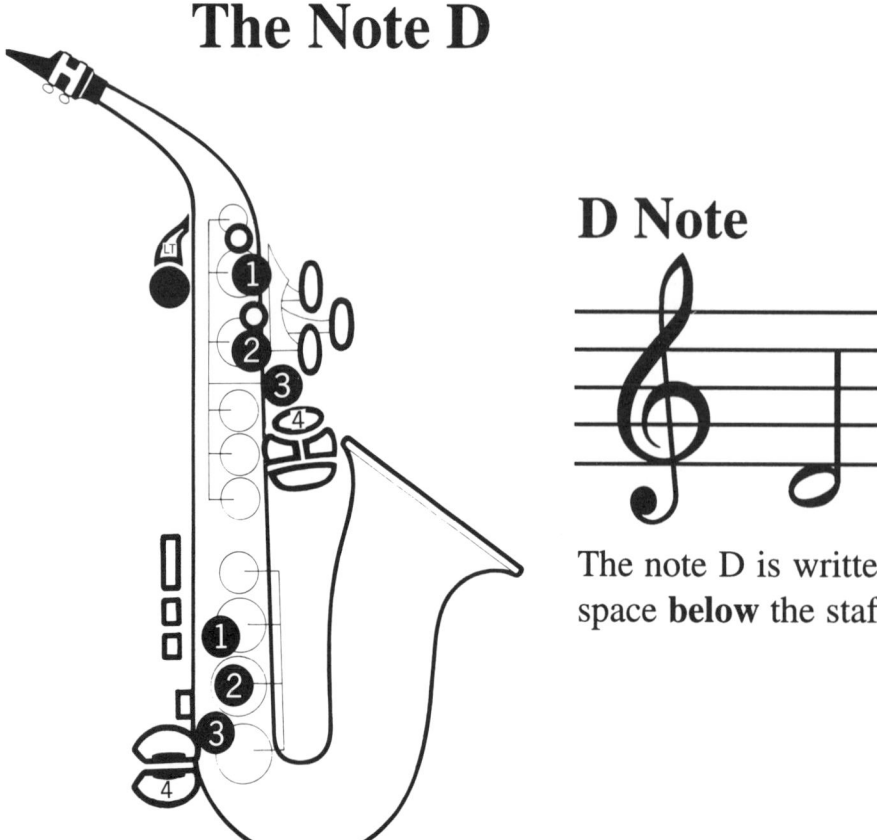

D Note

The note D is written in the space **below** the staff.

The Volga Boatman

Traditional Russian

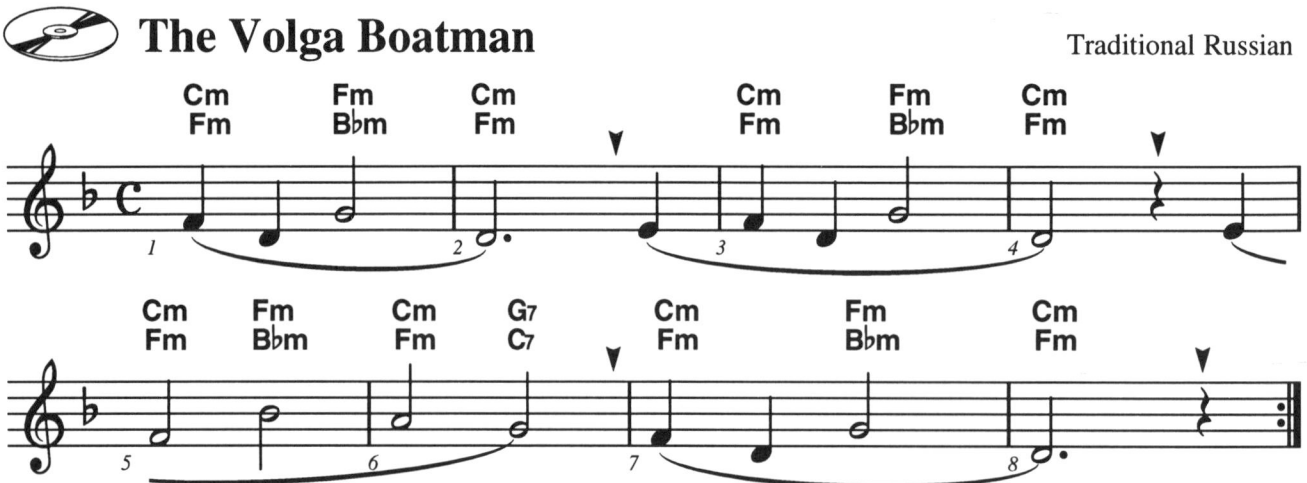

Harem Dance

On the recording there are **three** drumbeats to introduce this song.

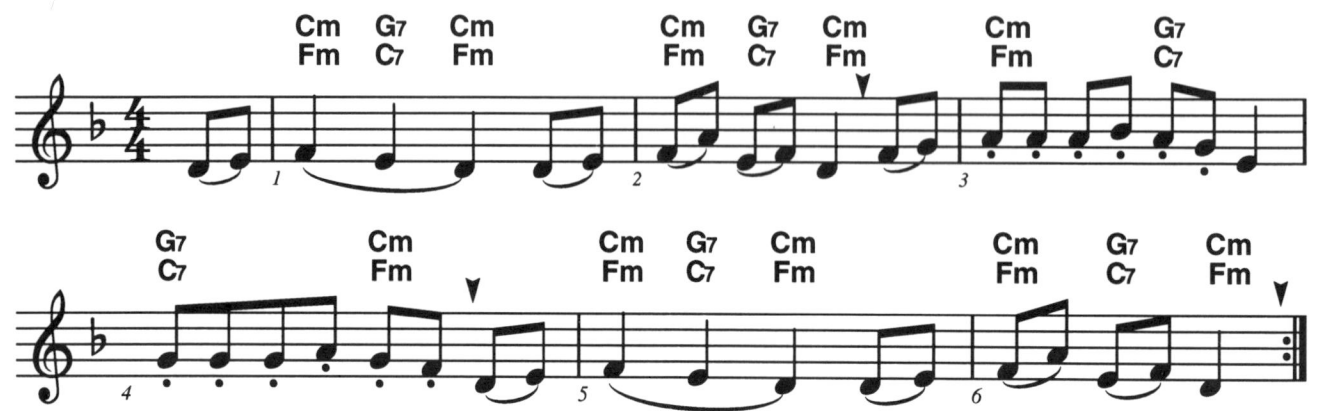

 **La Spagnola**

Traditional

 **How Dry I Am**

Traditional

On the recording there are **five** drumbeats to introduce this song.

You can now play the song There's a Hole in the Bucket, on page 5 of the Supplementary Songbook.

Lesson Eleven
The Note Low C

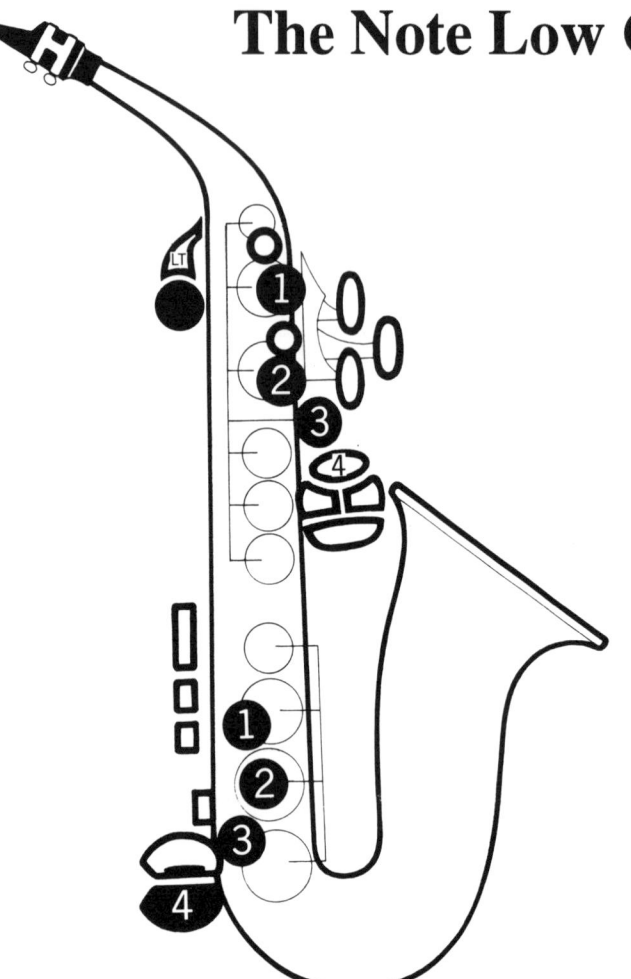

C Note

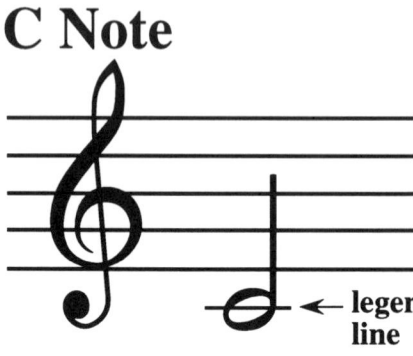

← leger line

Low C is written just below the staff on a short line called a **leger line**.

 ### Rock Riff 2

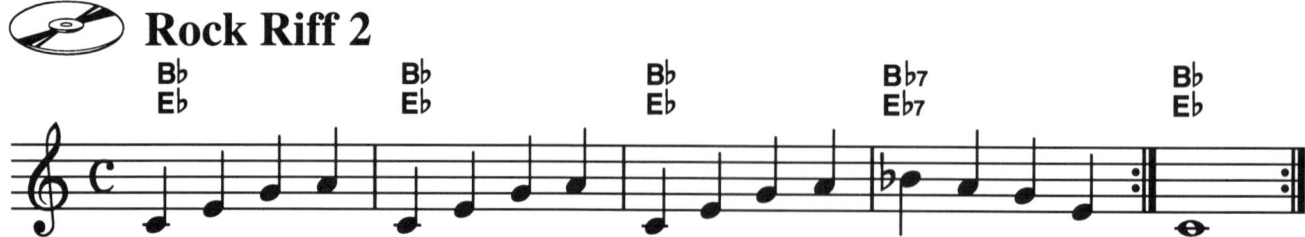

A flat sign after the treble clef also indicates the **key** (see glossary) of a piece. Sometimes, as in the next song, there is a flat sign even though there is no B note in the music.

The William Tell Overture

Giaochino Rossini

On the recording there are **three** drumbeats to introduce this song.

A Bicycle Built for Two

Traditional

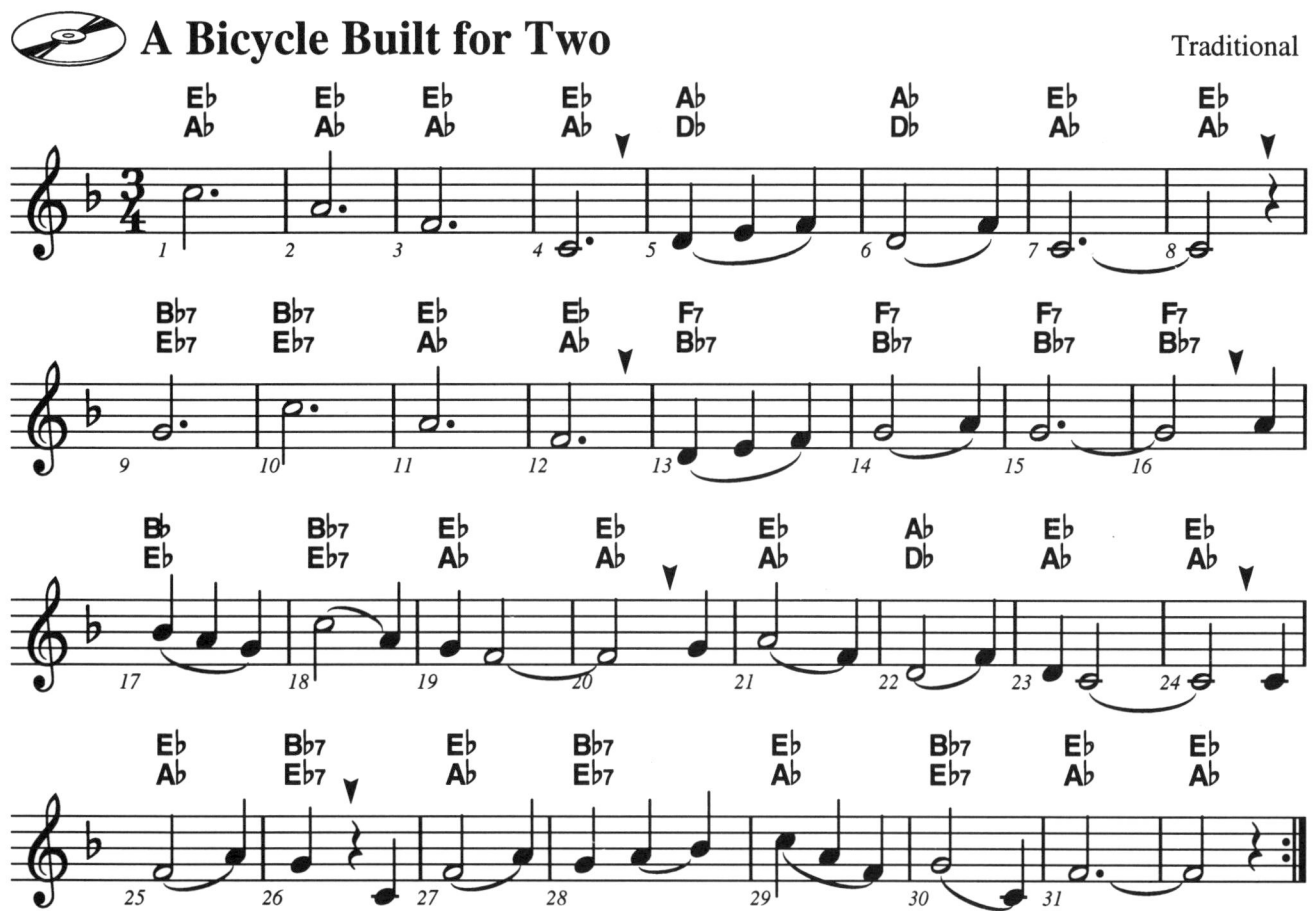

We Wish You a Merry Christmas

Traditional

On the recording there are **five** drumbeats to introduce this song.

The C Major Scale

A Major scale is a group of eight notes that produces the familiar sound:

Do   **Re**   **Mi**   **Fa**   **So**   **La**   **Ti**   **Do**

You now know enough notes to play the C Major scale:

C   D   E   F   G   A   B   C

 **Exercise 21**

The number underneath each note indicates its position in the scale.

The Octave

An **octave** is the range of eight notes of a **Major Scale**. The **first** note and the **last** note of a Major Scale always have the same name. In the C Major Scale the distance from Middle C to the C note above it (or C note below it) is one octave (eight notes).

1 Octave

Arpeggios

An **arpeggio** is the notes of a **chord** played one at a time. A chord is any three or more notes played together. Although you can't play chords on the saxophone, you can play the notes of a chord one at a time; that is, you play arpeggios.

A Major arpeggio is constructed from the **first**, **third** and **fifth** notes of a Major scale.

The C Major arpeggio uses the 1st, 3rd and 5th notes from the C Major scale - **C**, **E** and **G**. When you play a C Major arpeggio, you are playing the notes of a C chord.

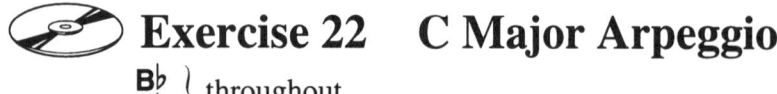 **Exercise 22**   **C Major Arpeggio**

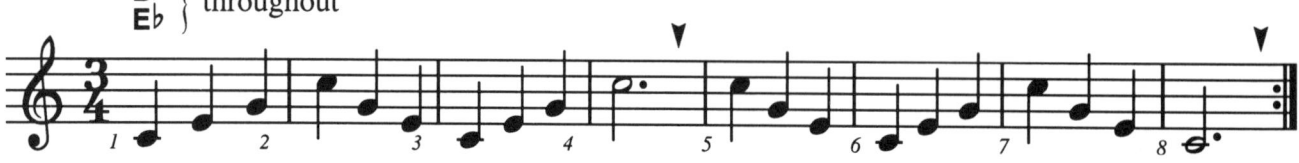

1st 3rd 5th notes of the scale.

 You can now play the songs For He's a Jolly Good Fellow and Aura Lee, on pages 5 and 6 of the Supplementary Songbook.

Lesson Twelve

The Dotted Quarter Note

A dot written after a quarter note means that you hold the note for **one and a half beats**. A dotted quarter note is often followed by an eighth note.

Exercise 23

Count   1   2   3   4   1   2   **+**   3   4   1   2   3   4   1   2   **+**   3   4

Turnaround in C

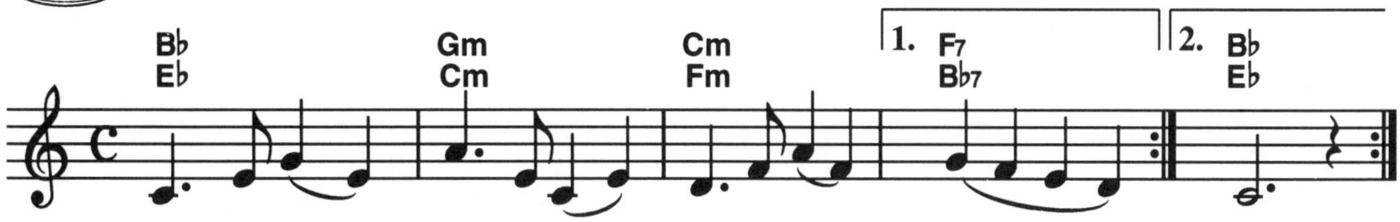

Home Sweet Home

Traditional

On the recording there are **three** drumbeats to introduce this song.

Count   1 2 3

Camptown Races

Stephen Foster

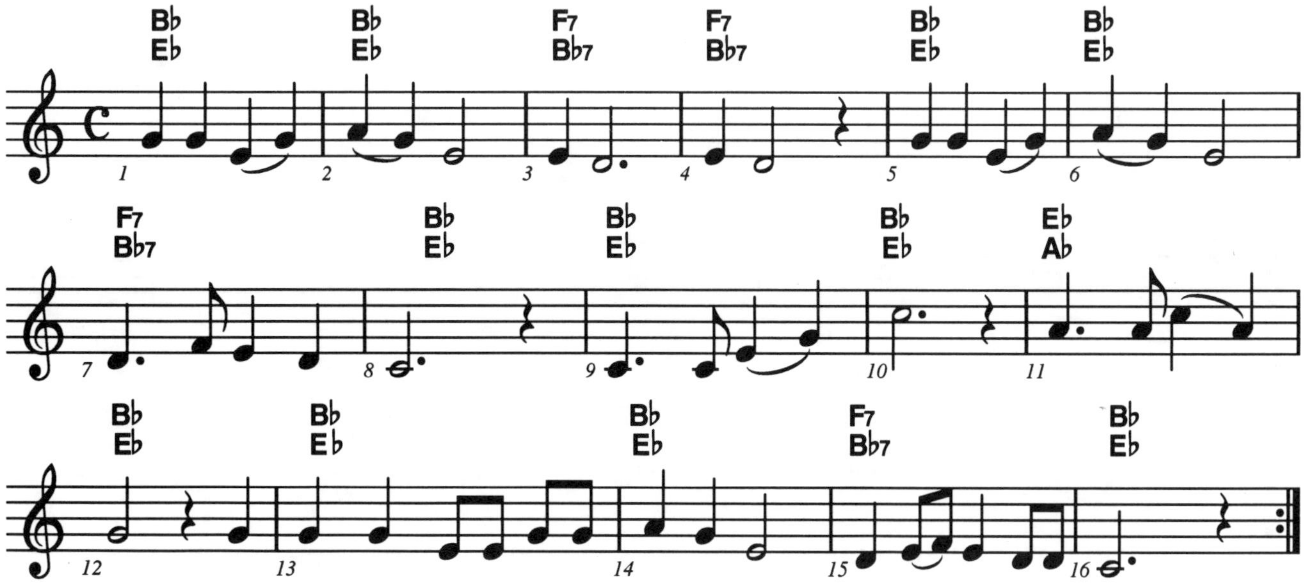

42

 **Muss i Den**

Traditional German

On the recording there are **six** drumbeats to introduce this song.

 **I Yi Yi Yi (Cielito Lindo)**

Traditional

On the recording there are **five** drumbeats to introduce this song.

You can now play the song Lullaby, on page 7 of the Supplementary Songbook.

Lesson Thirteen
The Note D in the Middle Register

D | 1 octave |

This D note is one octave higher than D in the low register.

The Registers of the Saxophone

A **register** on an instrument is a range of notes that have similar qualities of tone. On the saxophone there are four registers. All the notes you have learnt so far have been in the low register.

Octave key

To play the D note in the middle register use the same fingering as for D in the low register, and add the octave key. Remember to keep the ball of your left thumb on the thumb rest so that it can pivot on and off the octave key when required.

The Low Register
Bb to C#

The Middle Register
D to C#

The High Register
D to F#

The Altissimo Register
Above F#

Exercise 24

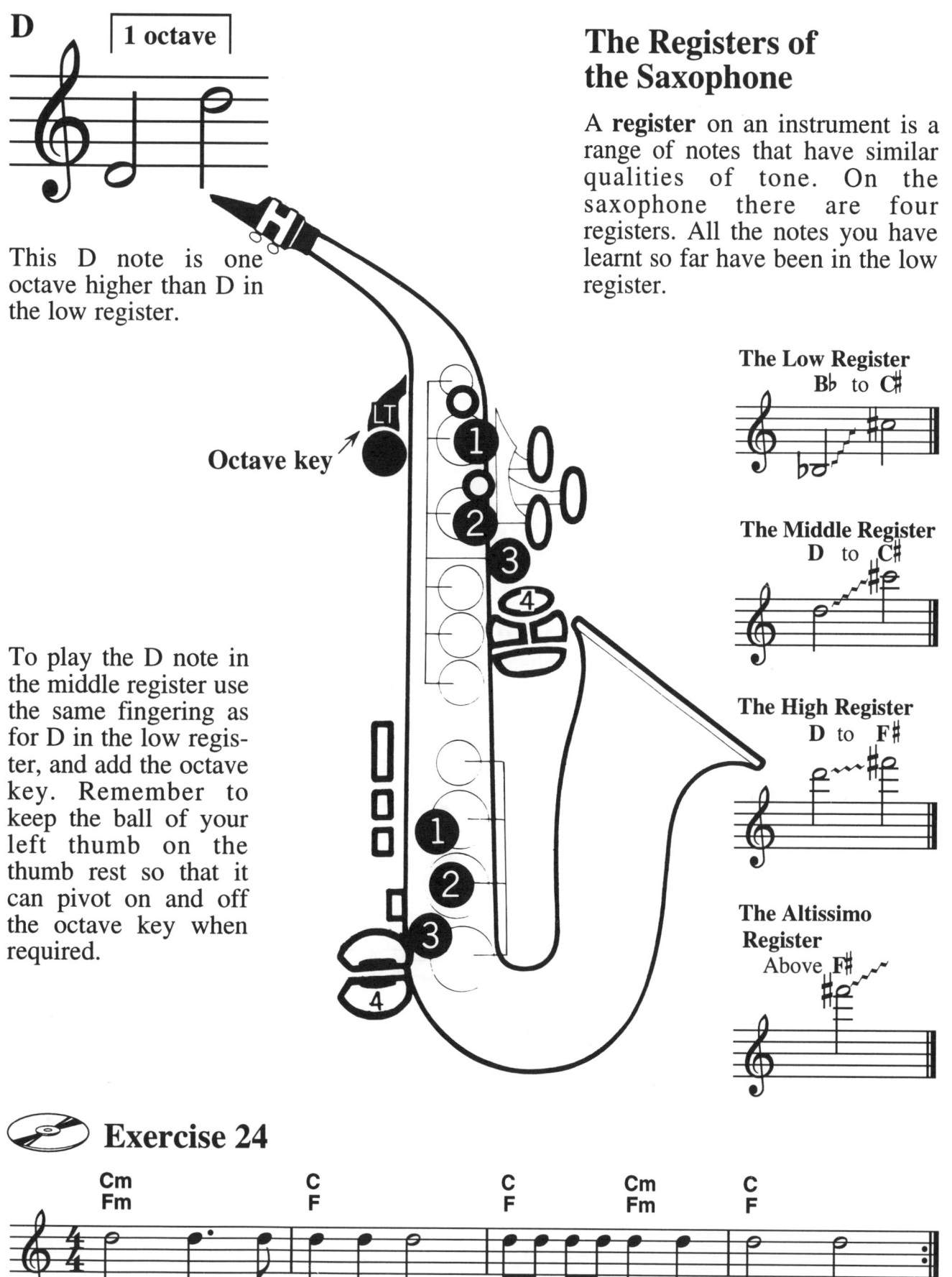

| Cm Fm | | C F | | C F | Cm Fm | C F |

Exercise 25

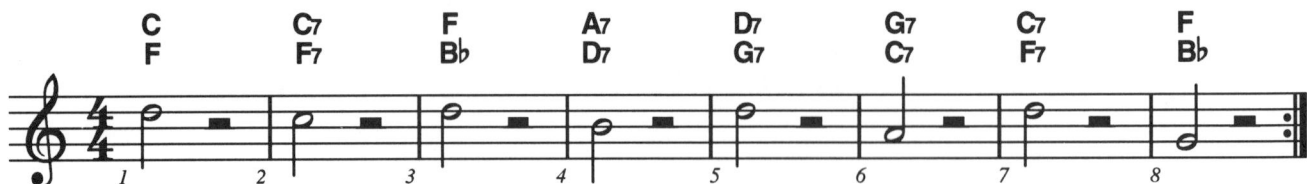

Exercise 26

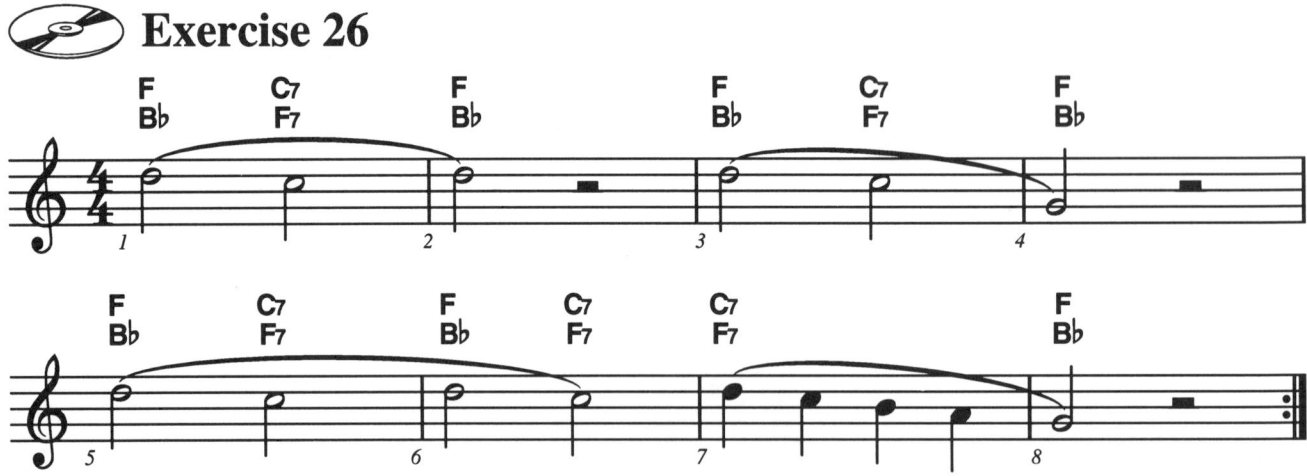

God Rest Ye Merry Gentlemen

Traditional

On the recording there are **three** drumbeats to introduce this song.

 **Auld Lang Syne** Traditional

On the recording there are **three** drumbeats to introduce this song.

 **Reveille** Traditional

On the recording there are **three** drumbeats to introduce this song.

Reeds

If you have been using a $1\frac{1}{2}$ strength reed, you may want to consider moving up to a 2 strength reed. By now your mouth muscles will have developed a little, and a stronger reed will give you a louder sound, and will respond better.

Look for reeds which are slightly green in color - the wood they are made from is young. Green-tinted reeds are more flexible than yellow ones, which tend to be a bit brittle. About 50% of reeds are unserviceable. It's not all your fault!

 You can now play the song Ode to Joy, on page 8 of the Supplementary Songbook.

Lesson Fourteen

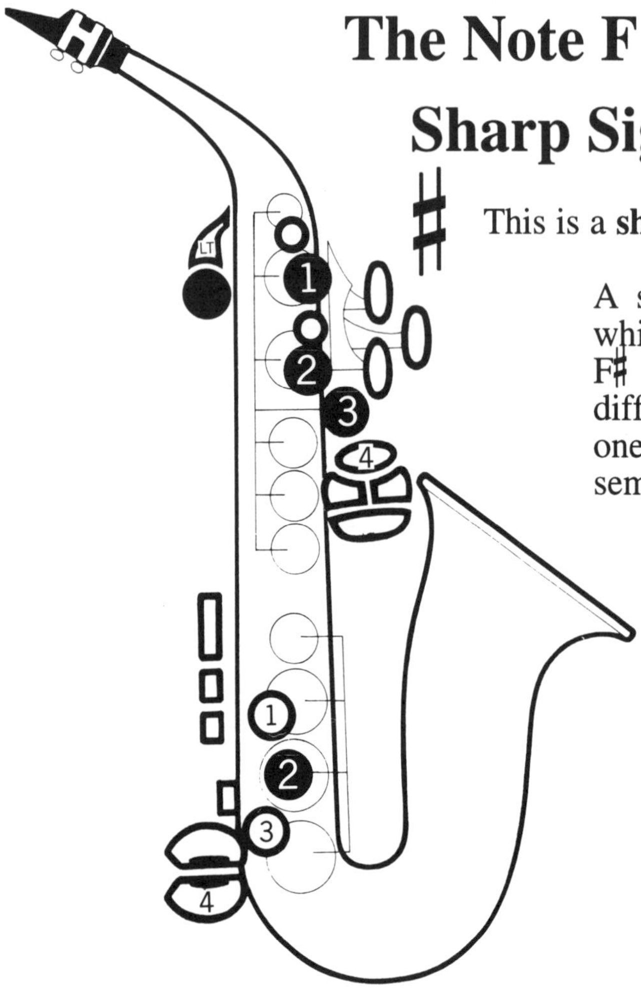

The Note F Sharp (F♯)

Sharp Signs

♯ This is a **sharp** sign.

A sharp sign raises the pitch of the note to which it applies by one semitone. Thus the note F♯ is one semitone **higher** than F. Since the difference in pitch between the notes F and G is one whole tone (two semitones), F♯ is also one semitone **lower** than G.

F♯ (F Sharp) Note

When a sharp note is written on the staff, the sharp sign is placed **before** the note.

🖸 Rock Riff 3

The sharp sign in bar 3 applies to both F's. (See "Accidentals" page 56).

🖸 Strike Up the Band

Traditional

 **Aloha Oe**

Traditional Hawaiian

On the recording there are **three** drumbeats to introduce this song.

Instead of writing a sharp sign before every F♯ note, it is easier to write just one sharp sign after the treble clef. This means that all F notes on the staff are played as F♯, even though there is no sharp sign placed before the note.

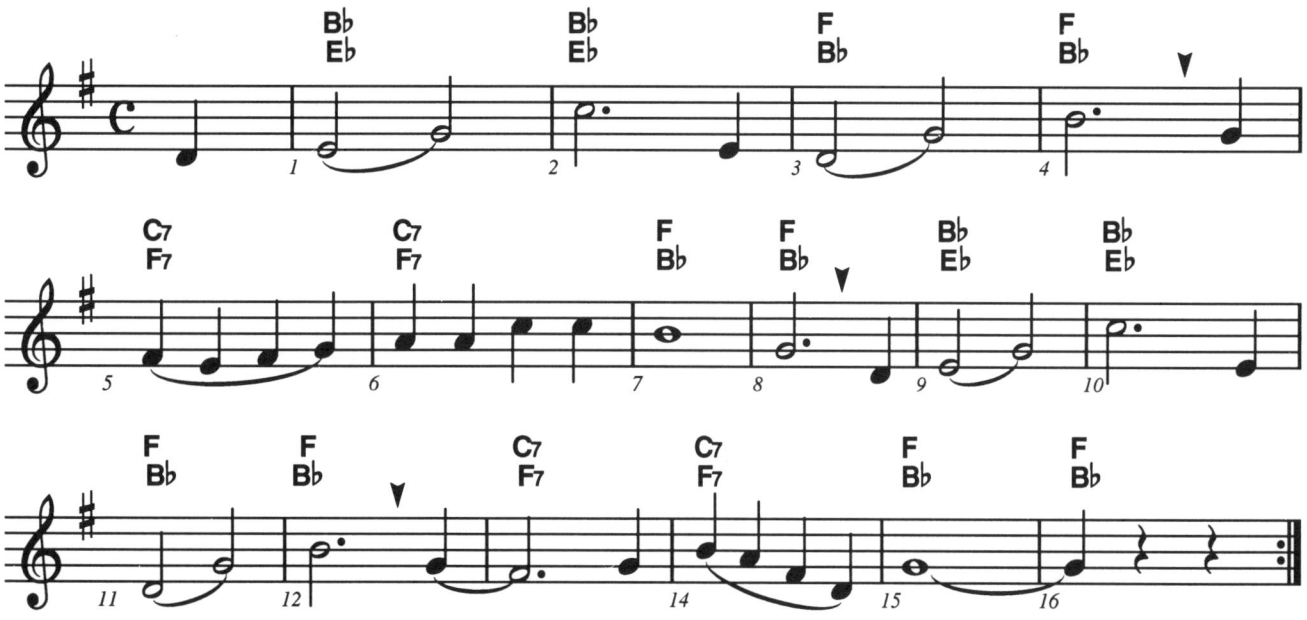

 **The Daring Young Man on the Flying Trapeze**

Traditional

On the recording there are **five** drumbeats to introduce this song.

 You can now play the song Ding Dong Merrily on High, on page 9 of the Supplementary Songbook.

Lesson Fifteen

The Note E in the Middle Register

On some makes of saxophone this note is a little higher in pitch than it should be. Listen carefully when you play with other instruments. If the note sounds sharp you can lower the pitch by loosening the pressure of your mouth on the reed.

E Note

The note E in the middle register is written in the **fourth** space of the staff.

Use the same fingering as for E in the low register, and add the octave key.

Exercise 27

4 O'Clock Rock

Hello My Baby

Traditional

♪ The Eighth Note Rest

This is an **eighth note rest** (or **quaver rest**). Its value is **half** a beat.

Exercise 28

The 1812 Overture

Peter Tschaikowsky

You can now play the songs on page 10 of the Supplementary Songbook.

Lesson Sixteen

The Note F in the Middle Register

F Note

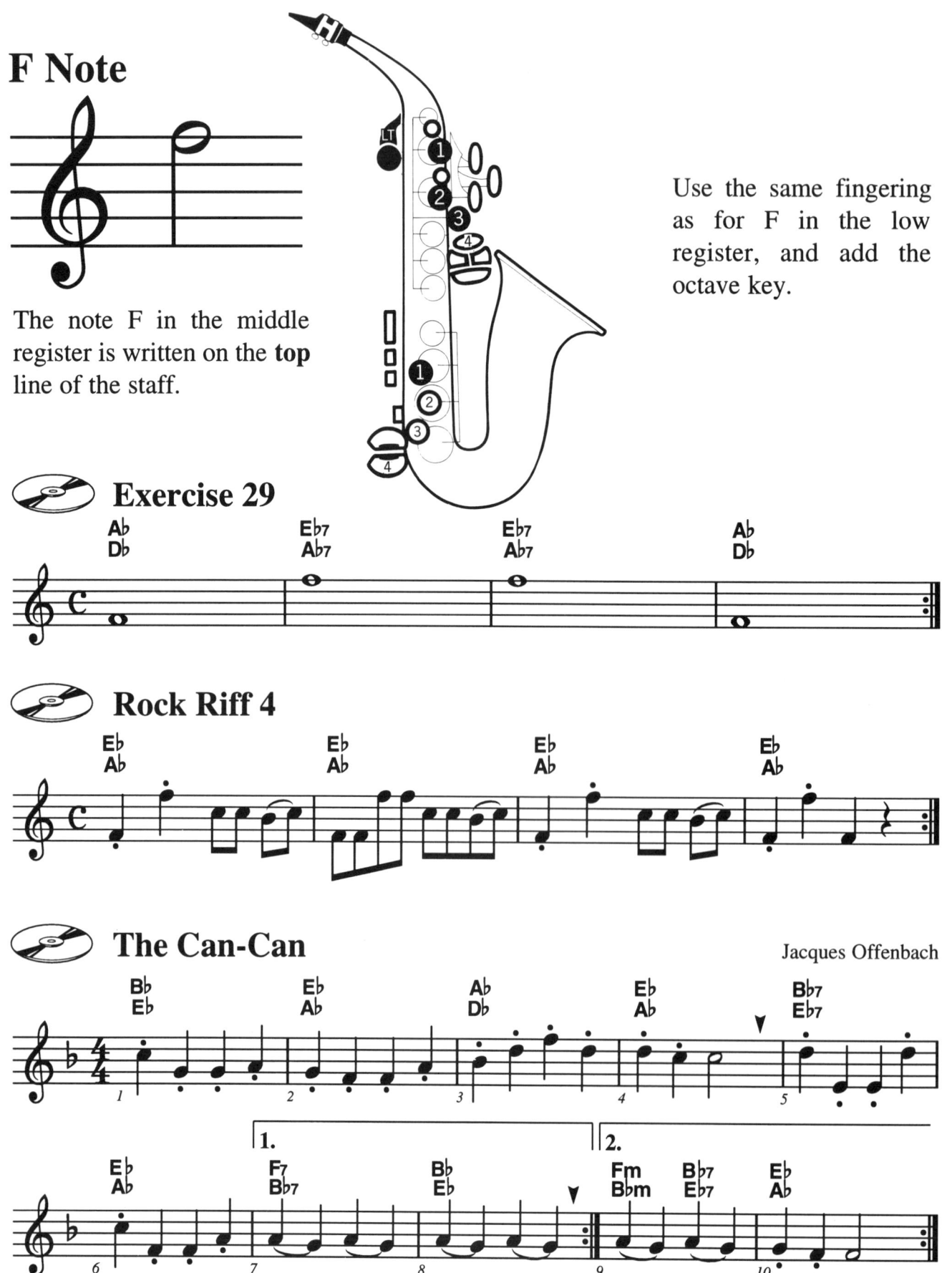

The note F in the middle register is written on the **top** line of the staff.

Use the same fingering as for F in the low register, and add the octave key.

Exercise 29

Rock Riff 4

The Can-Can

Jacques Offenbach

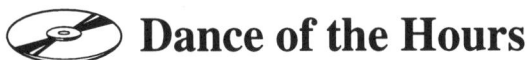 ## Dance of the Hours

A. Poinchelli

On the recording there are **three** drumbeats to introduce this song.

 ## Exercise 30　　The F Major Scale

The F Major scale contains one flat note - B♭. The flat sign for this B♭ note is usually written at the beginning of the staff, after the treble clef.

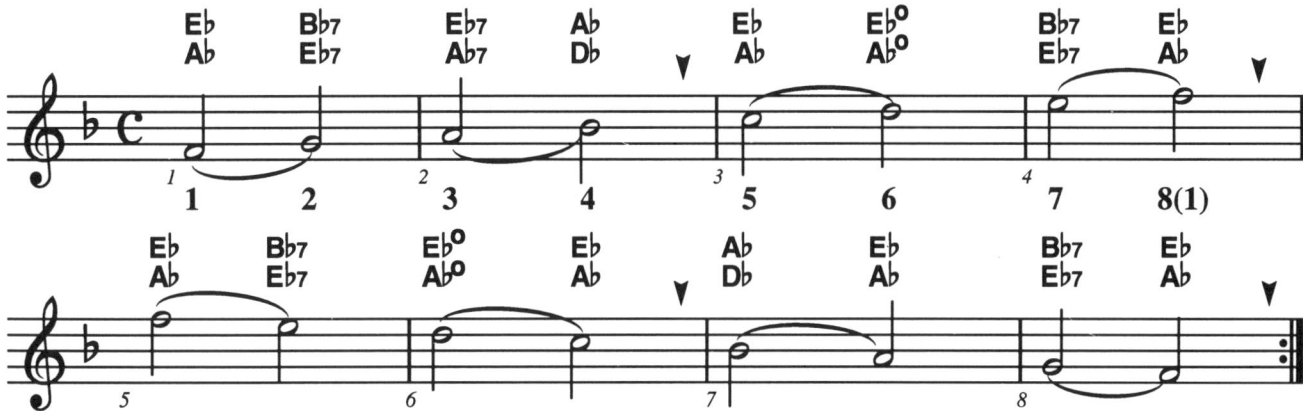

F Major Arpeggio

You have seen (in Lesson 11) that the C Major chord contains the first, third and fifth notes from the C Major scale, and that you could play a C Major arpeggio by playing the notes from that chord. The first, third and fifth notes from the F Major scale (F, A and C), when played together form the F chord. When you play them individually, these notes become an F arpeggio. When referring to a Major chord or arpeggio it is not always necessary to use the word "Major." "F arpeggio" means the F Major arpeggio, "C chord" means the C Major chord, and so on.

Exercise 31

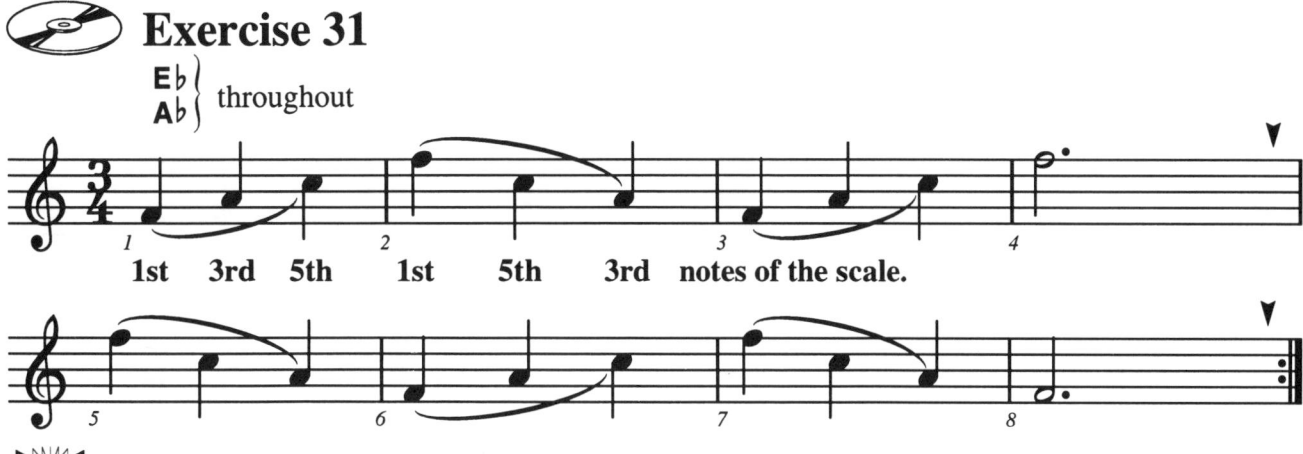

You can now play the songs on page 11 of the Supplementary Songbook.

Lesson Seventeen
The Note G in the Middle Register

G Note

The note G in the middle register is written in the **first space** above the staff.

Use the same fingering as for G in the low register, and add the octave key.

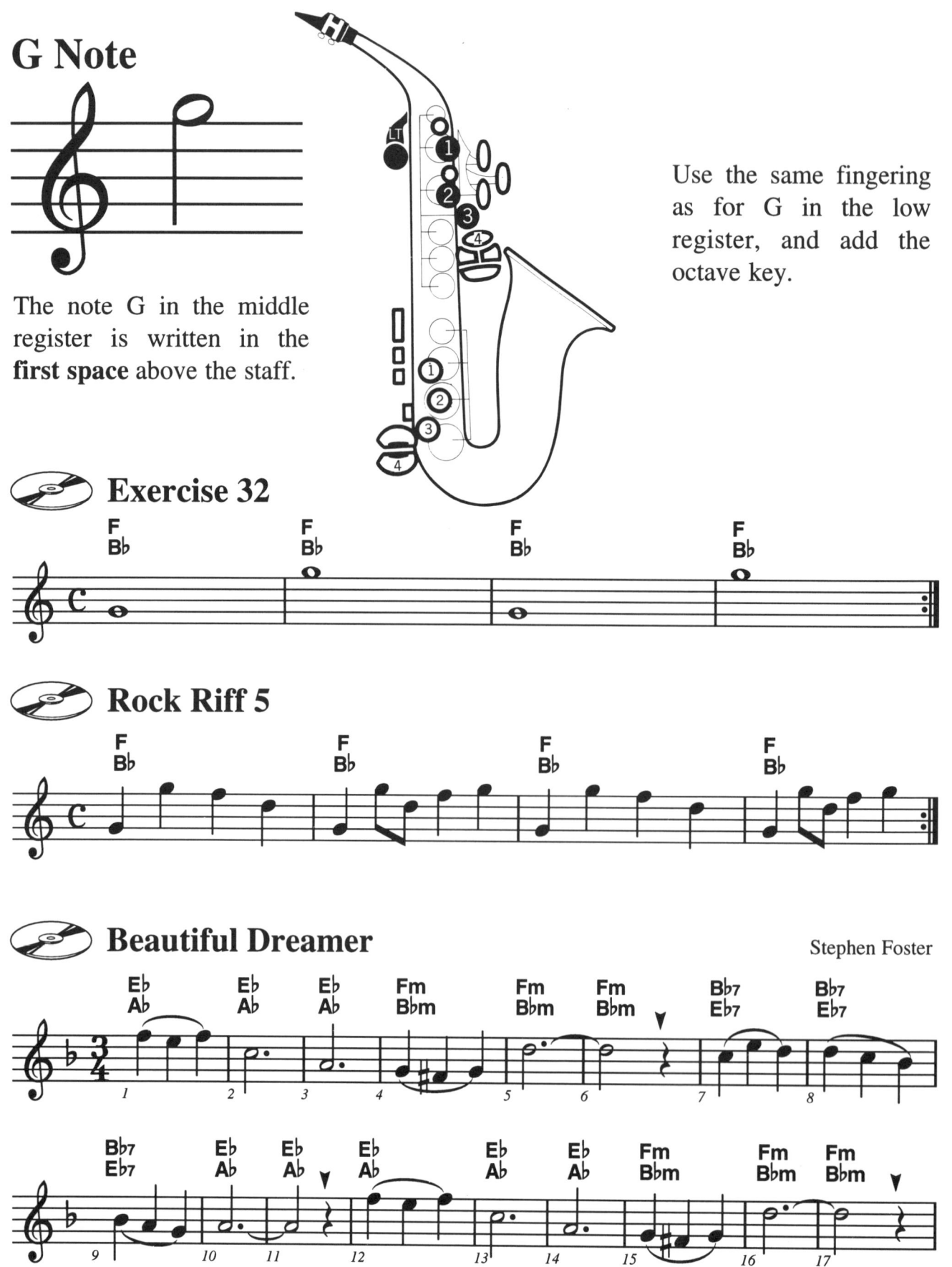

Exercise 32

Rock Riff 5

Beautiful Dreamer

Stephen Foster

 ## House of the Rising Sun

Traditional

On the recording there are **five** drumbeats to introduce this song.

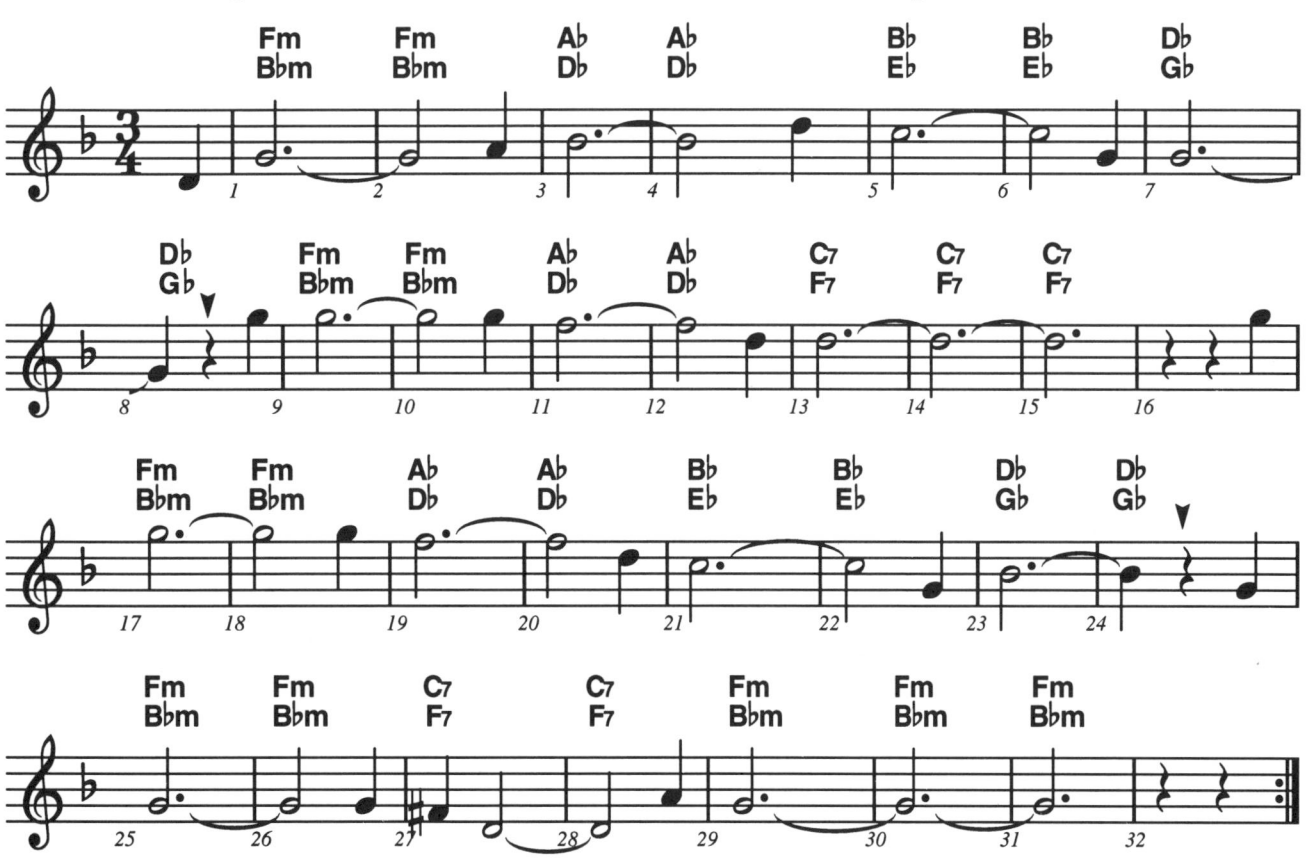

 You can now play the songs on page 12 of the Supplementary Songbook.

Lesson Eighteen

F♯ in the Middle Register

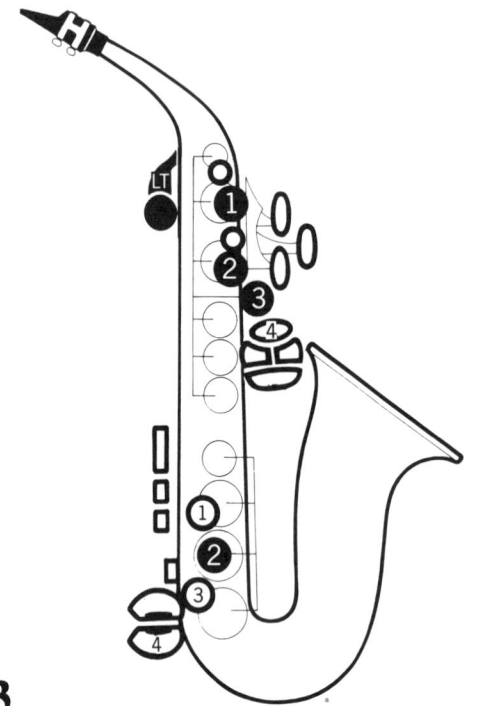

F♯ Note

Use the same fingering as for F♯ in the low register, and add the octave key.

 ## Exercise 33

The sharp sign after the treble clef applies to F notes in both the low and the middle registers.

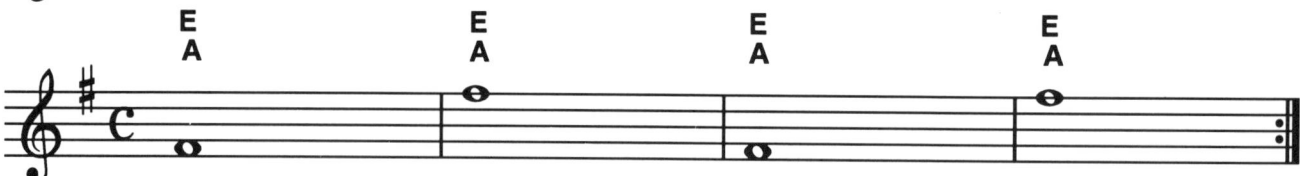

 ## Rock Riff 6

On the recording there are **four** drumbeats to introduce this song.

Sakura

Traditional Japanese

You now know enough notes to play the G Major scale.

The G Major scale contains one sharp note - F♯. The sharp sign for this F♯ note is usually written at the beginning of the staff, after the treble clef.

Exercise 34   G Major Scale

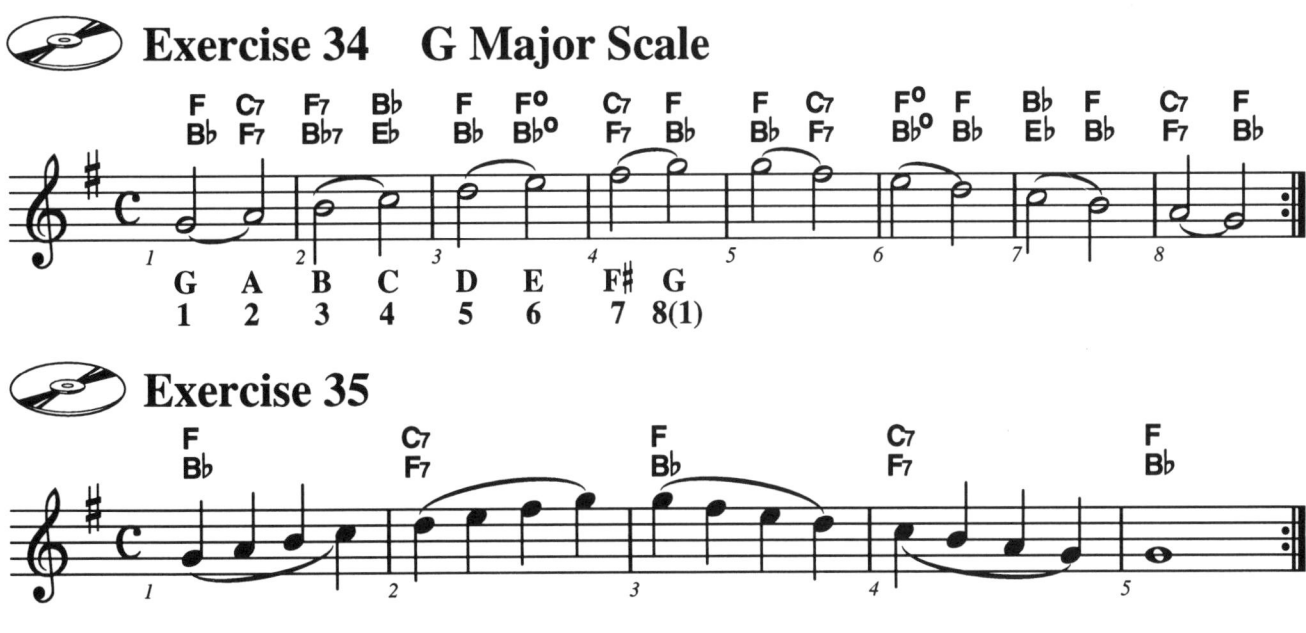

Exercise 35

G Major Arpeggio

You have seen (in Lessons 11 and 16) that the C and F chords consist of the first, third and fifth notes from the C and F Major scales respectively. The G chord contains the first, third and fifth notes from the G Major scale (G, B and D). When you play these three notes individually, you are playing the G arpeggio.

Exercise 36

 You can now play the songs on page 13 of the Supplementary Songbook.

Lesson Nineteen

Key Signatures

The number of sharp or flat signs after the treble clef is called the key signature. The key signature tells you which scale a melody is based on. So far you have played songs with three different key signatures.

Key of C Major — no sharps or flats

Key of F Major — one flat (B♭)

Key of G Major — one sharp (F♯)

There are many other key signatures based on major scales that you have not yet learnt. For more information on scales and keys, see Progressive Music Theory.

Accidentals

When a sharp or flat sign is written immediately before a note, and is not part of a key signature, the sign is called an **accidental**. Accidentals last for the whole bar E.g., the B♭ sign in bar 2 of Rock Riff 7 applies to both B notes. I.e., they are both played as B♭.

Rock Riff 7 in Key of C Major

The Natural Sign

This is a natural sign. A natural sign cancels the effect of a sharp or a flat. E.g. Rock Riff 8 is in the key of F major, which tells you to play all B notes as B♭. However, in bars 1, 2, and 3 there is a natural sign before the last B note in each bar. This natural sign cancels the effect of the key signature, and means that you play these notes as B instead of B♭.

Rock Riff 8 in Key of F Major

 Rock Riff 9 in Key of C Major

In this riff, accidentals are used to indicate that there are two B♭notes and one B♮ in each bar.

 12 Bar Blues in Key of C Major

This blues contains sharps, flats and naturals.

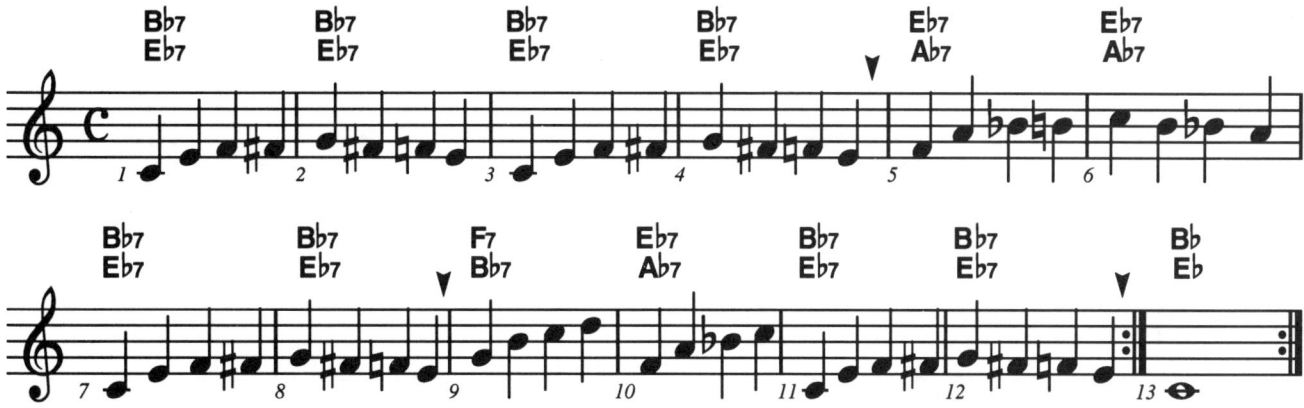

The Triplet

A triplet is a group of three notes played in the same time as two notes of the same kind. E.g., an **eighth note triplet** consists of three eighth notes played in the same time as you would play two eighth notes. Eighth note triplets are indicated by three eighth notes grouped together by a curved line and the numeral 3, as shown below. Triplets are easy to understand once you have heard them played. Listen to the recording.

 Exercise 37

Count   1   +   a   2   +   a   3   4   1   +   a   2   3   +   a   4

Exercise 38

1   2   3   +   a   1   2   +   a   3

58

Triplet March

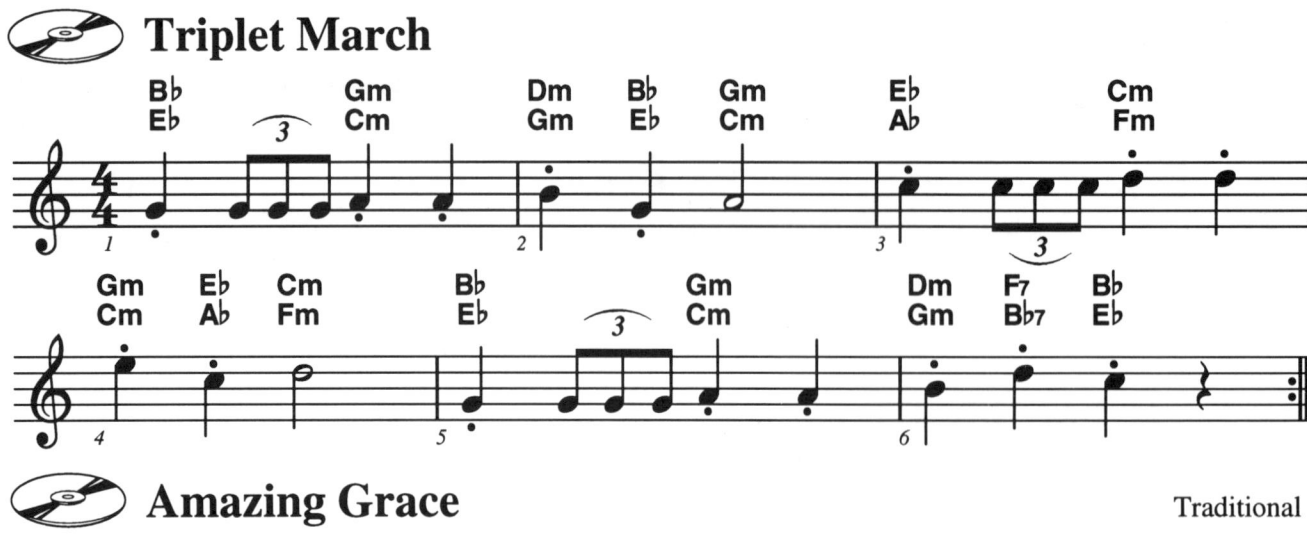

Amazing Grace

Traditional

On the recording there are **five** drumbeats to introduce this song.

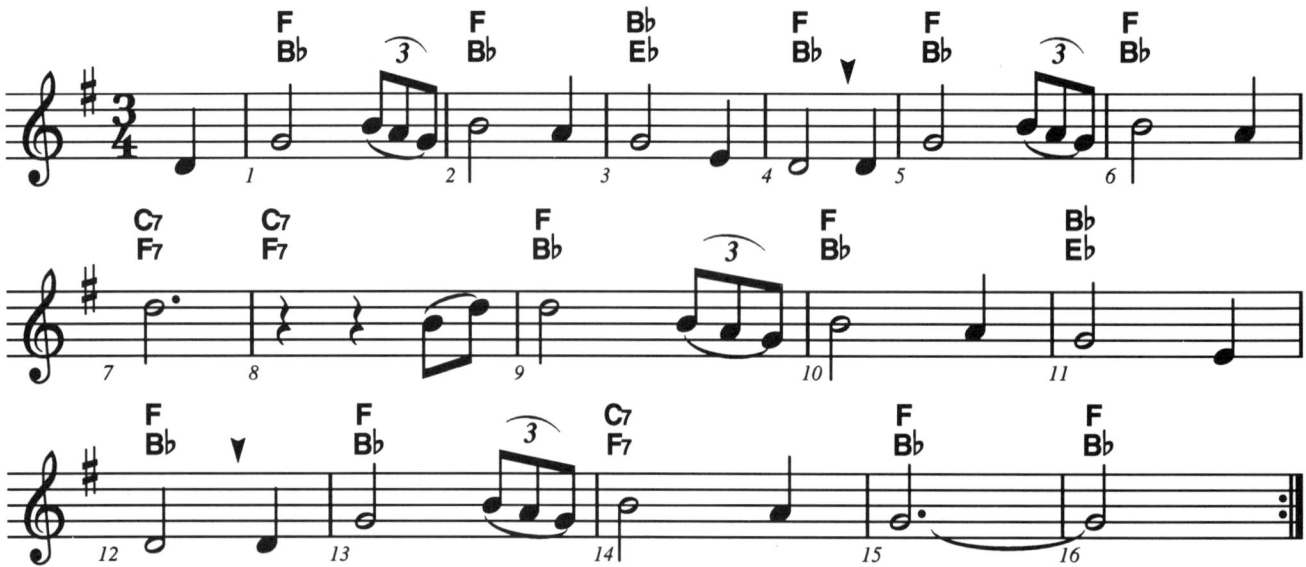

Swing Rhythms

A **swing rhythm** can be created by tying together the first and second notes of an eighth note triplet. Play Exercise 39a which contains standard triplets.

Exercise 39a

Play Exercise 39b which has the first and second notes of the triplet group tied. This gives the exercise a "swing feel".

Exercise 39b

 ## Exercise 39c

The two eighth note triplets tied together in Exercise 39b can be replaced by a quarter note.

To simplify notation, it is usual to replace the  ♩♪ with ♪♪ , 
and to write at the start of the piece, ♪♪ = ♩♪ as illustrated below in Exercise 39d.

 ## Exercise 39d

Exercises 39b, 39c and 39d sound exactly the same, but are just written differently.

Rock Riff 10

Swingin' the Blues

 **Creepy Blues**

This blues combines eighth notes with triplets in bars 9 and 10. The flat sign in bar 10 applies throughout the bar. Play this song as written, then play it with a swing rhythm.

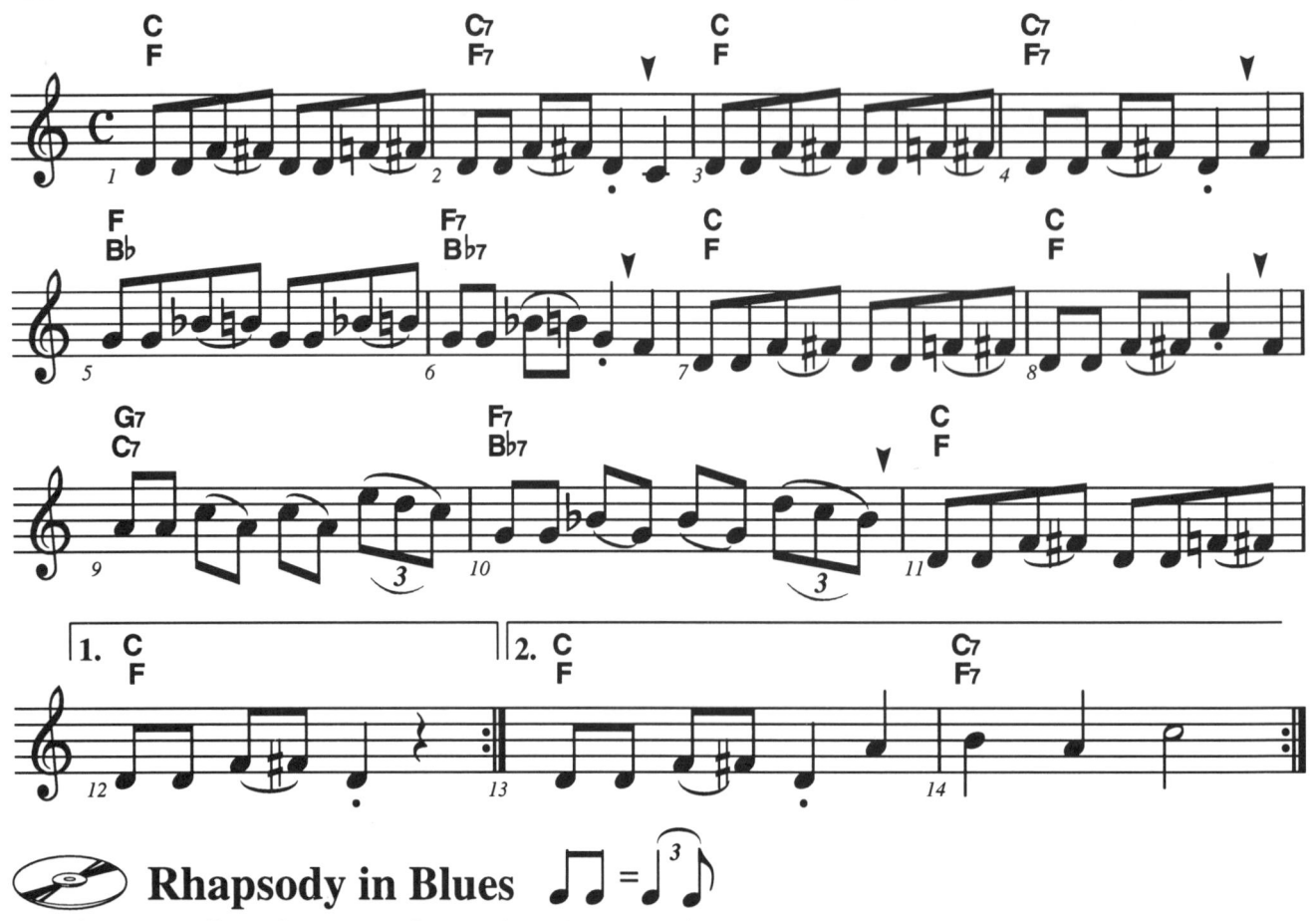

Rhapsody in Blues

On the recording there are **three** drumbeats to introduce this song.

You can now play the songs on page 14 and 15 of the Supplementary Songbook.

Glossary of Musical Terms

Accidental - a sign used to show a temporary change in pitch of a note (e.g. sharp♯ , flat♭, double sharp(✗) , double flat (♭♭) , or natural ♮). The sharps or flats in a key signature are not regarded as accidentals.

Arpeggio - the playing of a chord in single note fashion.

Augmented - term usually applied to the fifth note of a scale or chord and which means that the fifth is raised by one semitone.

Blues Scale - consists of the 1st, ♭3rd, 4th, ♭5th, 5th and ♭7th notes of a major scale.

Chord - a combination of three or more different notes played together.

Chromatic Scale - a scale ascending and descending in semitones. e.g. C chromatic scale:

ascending: C C♯ D D♯ E F F♯ G G♯ A A♯ B C
descending: C B B♭ A A♭ G G♭ F E E♭ D D♭ C

Diminished - term usually applied to the fifth note of a scale or chord and which means that the fifth is lowered by one semitone.

Double Flat - a sign (♭♭) which lowers the pitch of a note by one tone.

Double Sharp - a sign (✗) which raises the pitch of a note by one tone.

Embouchure - A French word that means the position of the lips when playing a wind or brass instrument.

Enharmonic - describes the difference in notation, but not in pitch, of two notes, e.g.

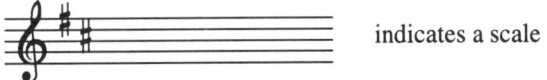

F♯ or G♭

Harmonic Minor Scale - type of minor scale which is produced by flattening the third and sixth notes of a major scale. E.g., the C Harmonic Minor scale - C, D, E♭, F, G, A♭, B, C - is the C Major scale with its third and sixth notes flattened.

Harmony - the simultaneous sounding of two or more different notes.

Improvise - to perform spontaneously: i.e. not from memory or from a written copy.

Interval - the distance between any two notes of different pitches.

Intonation - the art of making each note perfectly in tune.

Key - describes the notes used in a composition in regards to the major or minor scale from which they are taken: e.g. a piece "in the key of C major" describes the melody, chords, etc. as predominantly consisting of the notes C, D, E, F, G A and B - i.e. from the C scale.

Keynote - same as tonic, the note after which the key of a piece is named. E.g. in the key of F, the keynote is F.

Key Signature - a sign, placed at the beginning of each stave of music, directly after the clef, to indicate the key of a piece. The sign consists of a certain number of sharps or flats, which represent the sharps or flats found in the scale of the piece's key: e.g.

indicates a scale with F♯ and C♯, which is D major or B minor.

Melodic Minor - type of minor scale which features different notes in its ascending and descending sections. Produced by flattening the third note of a major scale for the ascending section, and using the flattened third, sixth and seventh notes for the descending section. E.g. the C Melodic Minor Scale, Ascending - C, D, E♭, F, G, A, B, C. Descending - C, B♭, A♭, G, F, E♭, D, C.

Metronome - a device which indicates the number of beats per minute, and which can be adjusted in accordance to the desired tempo. e.g. **MM** (Maelzel Metronome) ♩ = 60 - indicates 60 quarter note beats per minute.

Modulation - the changing of key within a song (or chord progression).

Natural Minor Scale - the most useful type of minor scale. Produced by flattening the third, sixth and seventh notes of a major scale. E.g., the C Natural Minor scale - C, D, E♭, F, G, A♭ , B♭ , C - is the C Major scale with flat third, flat sixth, and flat seventh notes.

Octave - the distance between any given note with a set frequency, and another note with exactly double or half that frequency. Both notes will have the same letter name: e.g.

A440   A880

1 Octave

Riff - a pattern of notes that is repeated throughout a song.

Semitone - the smallest interval used in western music.

Sixteenth Note - a note with the value of a quarter of a beat in ⁴⁄₄ time, indicated thus, ♪ (also called a semiquaver). The sixteenth note rest, indicating a quarter of a beat of silence, is written: ⅞

Syncopation - the placing of an accent on a normally unaccented beat: e.g.

$\frac{4}{4}$ > >
1 2 3 4

$\frac{3}{4}$ > >
1 + 2 + 3 +

Tempo - the speed of a piece.

Transposition - the process of changing from one key to another.

Unison - to sing or play in unison - to sing or play the same notes.

Vibrato - subtle fluctuations in a note's pitch, adding expression to long notes.

Fingering Index

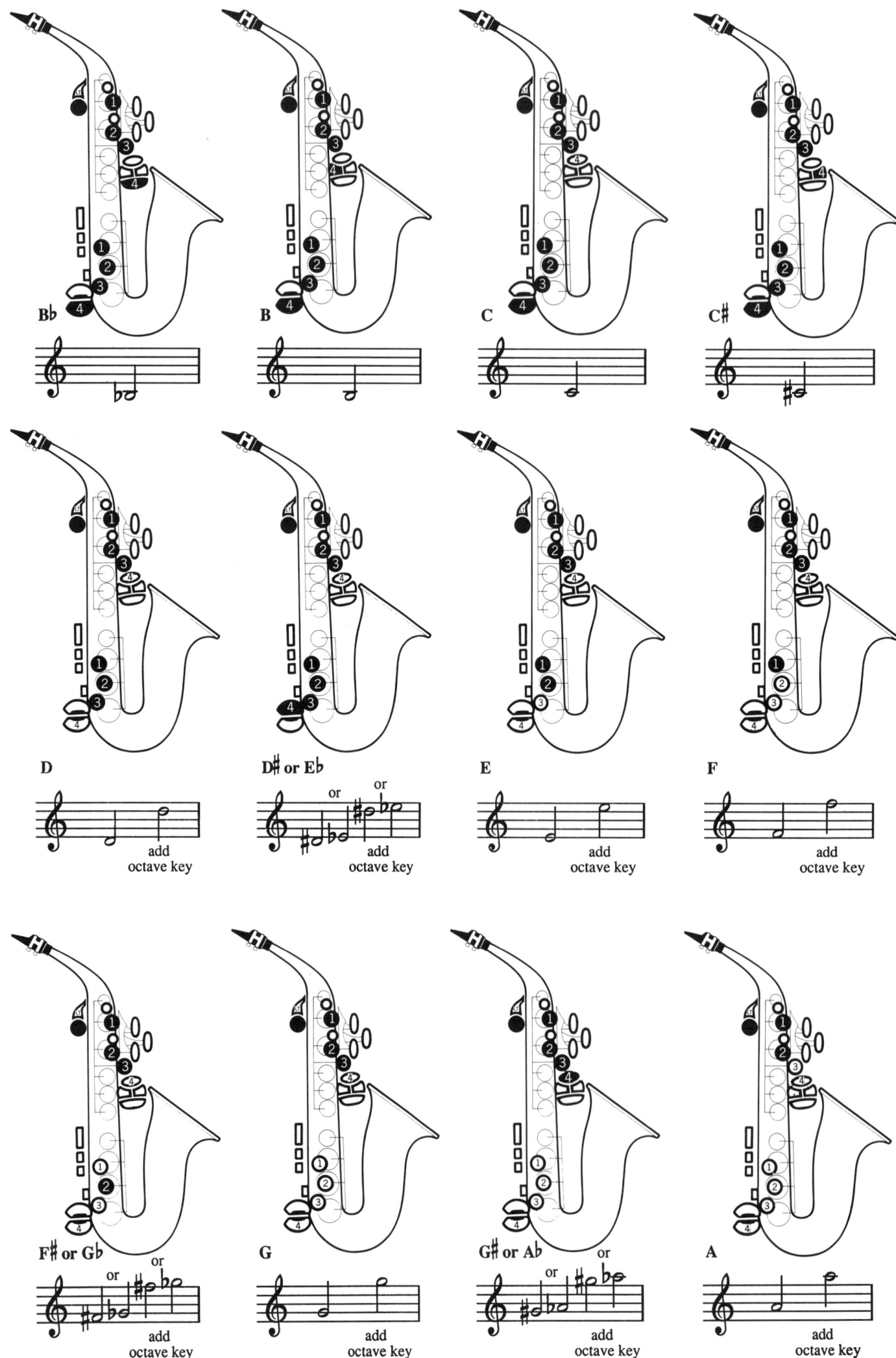

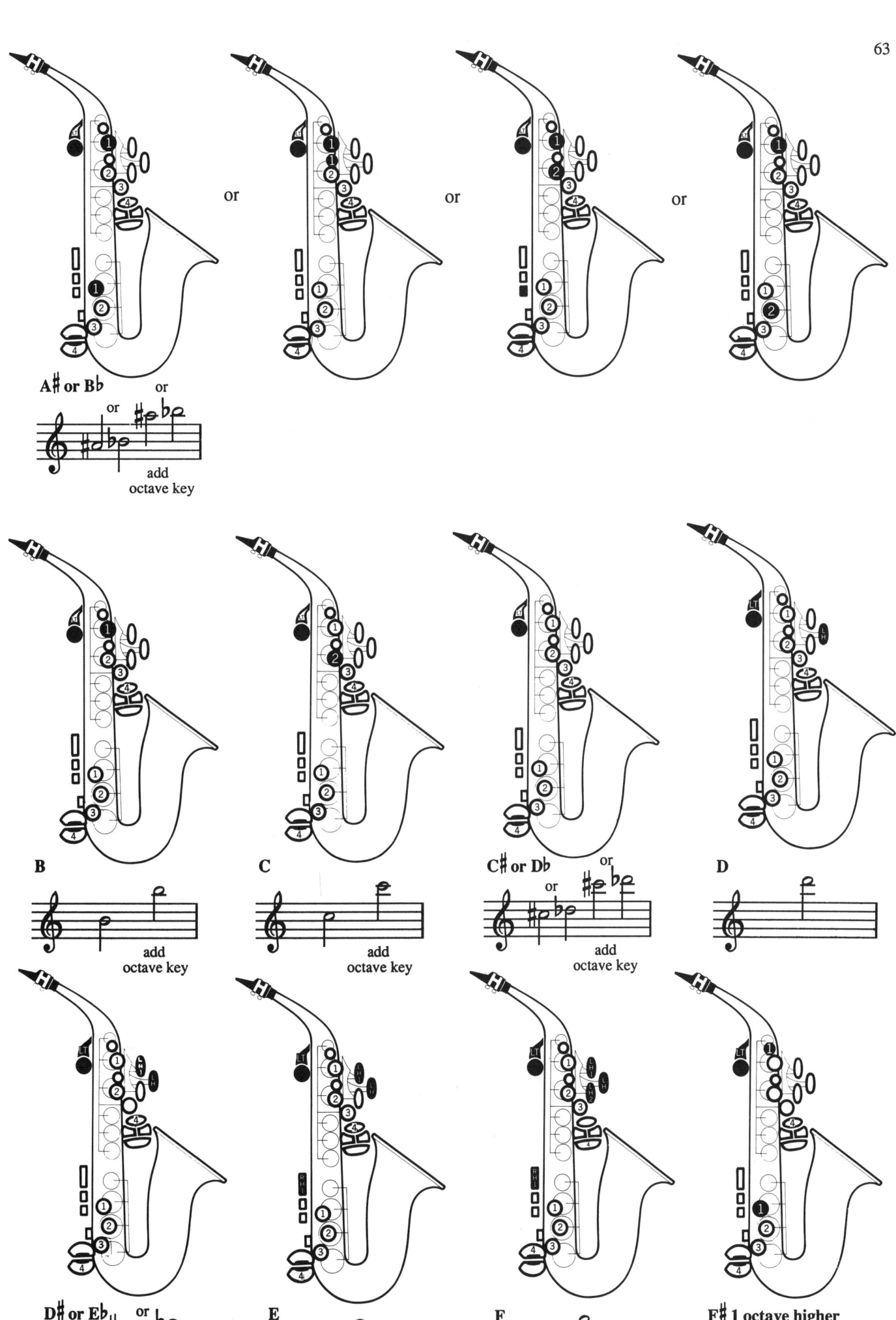

How To Play with Other Instruments

When you play a note on the saxophone, the sound it makes may be different to the sound produced by the same note on another instrument. For example, if you play a C note on the alto saxophone, a guitar would have to play an E♭ note for the two instruments to be producing the same sound. If you play a C note on the tenor saxophone, the guitar must play a B♭ note to produce the same pitch. This is why the saxophone is said to be a transposing instrument.

The chart below shows you which note you have to play in order to produce the same pitch as some other instruments. For example, if you want to play along with a guitarist, who is playing in the key of C, you must play in the key of A if you are using an alto sax, or in the key of D if you are using a tenor sax.

Transposing Chart

	E♭ Instruments Alto Sax Baritone Sax	**C or "Concert Instruments"** Guitar Piano Flute Violin	**B♭ Instruments** Tenor Sax Soprano Sax Clarinet Trumpet
Note or Key	C	E♭ or D♯	F
	C♯ or D♭	E	F♯ or G♭
	D	F	G
	D♯ or E♭	F♯ or G♭	G♯ or A♭
	E	G	A
	F	G♯ or A♭	B♭ or A♯
	F♯ or G♭	A	B
	G	B♭ or A♯	C
	G♯ or A♭	B	C♯ or D♭
	A	C	D
	B♭ or A♯	C♯ or D♭	D♯ or E♭
	B	D	E